Escape to Pearl City

By: Tephra Miriam

TEPHRAMIRIAM *Publishing*

TEPHRAMIRIAM *Publishing*, Chicago 60611

Text copyright © 2019 by Tephra Miriam

For information contact TEPHRAMIRIAM *Publishing*.

The publisher is not responsible for websites (or their content).

First edition 2019

Printed in the United States of America

Library of Congress Cataloging-in-Publication data on file.

ISBN: 978-1092198165

For all of those past and present that stand strong in the face of fear.

- Kayacum No Ai

ICE CREAM FIELDS

PRIMROSE PATH

DAIRY VILLAGE

GARDEN GATE VILLAGE

DARK FOREST

ICE CR

IRONSIDE MOUNTAINS

SEA OF FLOWE

CRYSTAL VA

WITCH KINGDOM

THE VALLEY OF SHADOWS

BOOK 2

In the Clown Town Adventures Series

TABLE OF CONTENTS

Prologue

The ringing in my ears won't stop. I hear a knock on a door. No, it's a hammer banging on a wall—but now it has stopped. I see something that hurts my eyes. It's the sun, yet it pains me now. Didn't I love the sun when I was a child growing up in the Garden Gate Village? I can't remember now...the sun...my home...my life...my dreams... I hear my mother call my name.

"Duchess, where are you sweet child?" she calls.
My eyes still hurt but are open to see the light...

I see the sun, I feel the earth, I feel each flower as I walk through a field of lilies. I shut my eyes to listen to the water's voice flow through my spirit. My feet feel the earth and the ground, yet I have no stinging pain of sharp rocks, nor do I feel the tiny legs of ants crawl across my toes. Am I awake? Am I really here? Is this death? I search for my mother but I only hear her voice. It's too much to take, so I shut my eyes to breathe in. When I open them again, my world has changed...

I can see my cottage just over the hill of green that I tumbled down as a child. The memory of my village life seems like a dream that I had many years ago. Now I hear voices and see the dark dances of sorcerers that have harvested the essence of my soul.

I was so unhappy for so long as a child, even though I was surrounded by the beauty of the earth that those on high gave to humanity long ago. I dreamed of a life that was not meant for me. I loved a man that hated me. I lived a lie that will haunt me forever.

Now I head into the unknown without knowing who I am. What I once knew as love I now fear. My world...it changes. It shifts like the eyes of a lion stalking its prey. I close my eyes in fear, hoping to wake up but I can't. I'm caught in his lair. I've heard his voice many times. I still hear it echoing in my head. He calls to his conjurers, to his soldiers and to all of darkness to come to him and bow before him.

I scream at him, "What am I to do with the world's dark destiny? Tell me!"

I've chased him in my dreams yelling that I am only a village girl. What have I to do with the end of the world!? Please...please...please let me go. In every dream, Epsilon turns to me and says, "The world can be overthrown by an army of ants. Its destiny is in the hands of the abandoned, yet they do not know it nor act upon it."

I will never be who I once was.

1

Heaven Help Us

Duchess' legs burned from running. Her lungs felt tight, and her eyelids felt heavy from lack of sleep.

"Hurry Duchess, hurry."

Duchess looked over at Chewy, the large purple gumdrop running beside her in despair. Her head wouldn't stop pounding, and sweat began to burn her eyes. *I must be dreaming*, she thought to herself. The sound of General Sharaya's voice quickly reminded her that she was very much awake.

"Duchess, keep up!" Shouted General Sharaya as she took the lead. She slashed at any branch that stood in her way with her sword, clearing a path for Duchess and Chewy. The chubby gumdrop huffed and puffed as she tried to keep up with the two humans.

All Duchess could remember was lying on a hard cement floor in the dark dungeon of Clown Town.

"General, please... I can't...I can't breathe. Please, I need to rest just for a moment."

General Sharaya slowed her pace, reached for a leather pouch filled with water and gave it to her.

"Here, drink this. Thank heavens...thank heavens," the General breathed quietly.

Duchess tried hard to catch her breath and wiped tears from her eyes at the thought of Truffles.

"What do you think they'll do to him? We have to do something!"

General Sharaya stayed silent while her tired eyes stared coldly into the dark forest.

"Come on, we need to keep moving. We must get to Sugar Valley before daybreak. We need to leave this place as soon as possible and escape to Pearl City."

One Hour Earlier...

Truffles watched Jax walk wearily back into the palace and disappear behind the large palace doors. His heart pounded, and his mouth felt dry. He knew that it was now or never and that the deylai could come for him at any moment. Truffles gripped Duchess' star stone that he had hidden in his pocket and took a deep breath. By the time he had gotten out of the car, his classic clown smile was perfectly pasted on his face.

"Good evening soldier," he said cheerfully while walking into the palace.

Truffles tried his best to steady his nerves. His thoughts turned to what he had done back at the Conjurer's cottage, where he had been forced to make a quick decision. He went inside and spoke to the Conjurer's maid but left quickly without seeing him. Thoughts raced through his mind. *I shouldn't have deceived Jax but what else was I to do? Everyone around here seems to have gone mad.*

Truffles walked through the main hall of the palace until he reached a small stone doorway that the servants often used. He descended down the dark stairs and walked through a cold dark tunnel that led to the dungeon. *What shall I say to the guards? Um...uh, I could tell them that Jax...no, that the Conjurer wants me to check on the prisoners. Yes. That should do it.*

Tears suddenly welled up in his eyes. *I only pray that I'm not too late*, he thought. He took a deep breath while he rounded the last dark corner that led to the dungeon. Truffles shuddered at the sound of prisoners shouting and cries of pain in the distance. Despite his drumming heartbeat, he walked confidently up to the clown guards that stood in front of Duchess and General Sharaya's cell and cleared his throat loudly.

"Good evening gentleclowns. I'd like to see the prisoners if I could please. Straight away."

"We been instructed not to let anyone see to 'em yer Lordship."

"Do you dare to defy me? My orders come directly from... Epsilon. Now open this door at once and go fetch chains for them! We are moving the prisoners to the Conjurer's cottage tonight."

The clown guards scurried to do as they were told. As soon as the guards were out of sight, Truffles rushed into the prison cell and found Duchess lying on the floor in General Sharaya's lap.

"Duchess, can you hear me sweetheart? It's me Sharaya. Please open your eyes, I beg you."

Truffles rushed to Duchess' side, placed his hand on her forehead and stroked it gently.

"Don't touch her! Get away!" Yelled General Sharaya—pushing Truffles away.

Truffles stared helplessly at Duchess.

"What's happened to her?"

"Don't pretend to be daft, clown. You and your kind have ripped out her star stone and plan to deliver her to Epsilon so that he can consume her blood. Now get back!"

"I have it. I have her star stone. Here take it...please...take it and make her well," he cried.

Truffles removed the stone from his pocket and handed it to General Sharaya. She quickly took the stone and laid it on

Duchess' chest. The General bowed her head and squeezed her eyes tightly while she spoke in the old Farish tongue.

"Mun haya nanoee. Let the light of heaven guide you back to the ones you love."

The dark dungeon was silent as the grave for what felt like an eternity. Truffles trembled watching Duchess' cold and still body lying motionless on the stone floor. General Sharaya held the stone closer to Duchess' chest and spoke louder.

"Mun haya nanoee! It can't be too late. It just can't be. Felanthiam if you can hear me, please help us...heaven help us!"

Truffles and General Sharaya stared helplessly at Duchess with tears and sweat running down their faces when the stone began to glow. General Sharaya let go of the stone when it started to attach itself to Duchess' skin and sank slowly into her chest until it disappeared. Duchess suddenly gasped for air and began to cough.

"Duchess! Thank heavens! Oh, thank heavens!" General Sharaya exclaimed.

"We thought we'd lost you, dearie. Quick now. I have to get you both out of here," said Truffles. "The guards will return at any moment."

Truffles helped General Sharaya get Duchess to her feet. They stumbled from the cell, with Truffles leading the way down the dark corridor of the dungeon. The cold dungeon air quickly helped Duchess come to her senses, and she started to regain her strength.

"Truffles, is that you? What are you doing?" She gasped. "Epsilon will...he'll have you...killed for helping us. You must... you must come with us."

The thought of leaving Clown Town had never occurred to him until just then.

"Did you hear me Truffles? They will kill you," repeated Duchess. "You must come with us to...to...wherever we're going."

"Don't worry about me, dearest. We need to get you out of here. Hurry now. I can hear the guards coming."

The lights from the guards' torches lit up the dark corridor as they drew closer behind the trio.

"There they are gents!" A clown soldier yelled. "After them!"

Truffles, Duchess, and General Sharaya reached the end of the dark corridor and started up a long stairwell.

"How do you plan to get us out of the palace, Truffles? King Clownington would die before letting us walk out the front door," barked General Sharaya.

"I uh, haven't quite gotten that far yet. There must be a back way out of here."

"Well, where is it? We are sitting ducks in this stairwell!" General Sharaya hissed.

"Wait a minute. I smell food. We must be near the kitchens. Quickly, follow me. There has to be a way out this way."

Truffles led the way through the door to the kitchen. The clown cooks were busy cooking and barely noticed them. The three made it through the kitchen and finally reached the back door. Truffles exited the kitchen first and ran straight into two royal clown guards. Duchess and General Sharaya quickly pulled back into the kitchen and slid into a dark corner before the guards saw them. The two guards rose to attention when they saw Truffles.

"Uh, kin we be o' any 'elp yer Lordship? Pardon me sayin' but yer lookin' quite uh troubled."

"No, no thank you. I came down here to...fetch...you both. It seems that a couple of prisoners have escaped, and all guards must report to the main floor at once."

"Yes sir. We' been alerted an' were told to stay posted 'ere yer Lordship. We 'ave also been told that one of our own 'as betrayed us."

The clown guards' eyes grew dark with suspicion.

"Yeh wouldn't 'appen to, eh know about any o' this would yeh yer Lordship?"

"Why I never! That's the most preposterous thing I've heard all day. Of course not. I'll accompany both of you myself to the main floor. They have asked for you. It will be your heads if you disobey General Madix's orders."

"Uh, yes sir. Sorry, sir. We'll come right away yer Lordship."

"No! You ca...," Duchess started to shout.

General Sharaya placed her hand over Duchess' mouth and grabbed onto her, pulling her back into the corner. Duchess tried hard to reach for Truffles but could not escape the General's grasp. Truffles looked toward the dark corner where he knew Duchess and General Sharaya were hiding while he began to follow the guards to the main floor. He smiled even though his eyes were filling with tears and mouthed one word in silence.

"Run."

As soon as the guards were out of sight, General Sharaya grabbed onto Duchess' arm and dragged her from the kitchen. The two sprinted across the cobblestone alley toward the edge of the dark forest behind the palace. The closer that they came to the forest, the more a small, purple gummy-looking figure holding a small candle and a leather pouch came into view.

"General, what is that?"

"Thank heavens!" the General exclaimed. "Zionous must have sent a message to the Twills of Normandeery. We will take refuge in Sugar Valley until we can find a way home."

On the Palace Main Floor

Truffles knew that it was of no use to run. If the clowns didn't find him, the deylai surely would. The main floor of the palace was heavily guarded and swarming with both royal clown guards and deylai soldiers. In the center of the large main floor stood the royal family along with the Conjurer and General Madix. Truffles shivered just looking at the General. The scarred indentations on his face were often filled with cakey clown makeup that always made Truffles feel squeamish. Truffles huffed in and out slowly as if they were his last breaths. As Truffles drew closer, he met Jax' gaze and saw that his eyes were red with anguish.

"Tell me it isn't true Truff. Tell us all that you didn't steal the star stone and help Duchess and General Sharaya escape," said Jax. "Are you mad? Do you know what Epsilon has ordered? He's commanded a fate worse than death for the clown who has helped them escape."

General Madix stared at Truffles coldly.

"Yes. The young prince is quite correct, unfortunately. Epsilon has ordered that the one responsible for helping them escape must be swiftly sent to Master Druix. Have yeh 'eard of him? I me self 'ave only 'eard stories about the dungeons of Witch Kingdom an' the incantations of Master Druix. The prisoners there dare not even speak his name. He 'as the power to torture yer soul beyond the grave some say. A very dark destiny awaits yeh, yer Lordship. I hope that yer sacrifice for those two fairies was worth yer while." Said General Madix.

He chuckled which sent a shiver up everyone's spine; even King Clownington's.

"Why Truff? Why risk your life just for them?" Asked Jax.

Truffles stood motionless. The moment seemed to be unreal. He knew now that there was no going back and no one to rescue him.

"Loving someone more than you love yourself can make one do insane things I guess. A clown should never forsake a friend."

2

The Secret Clown Militia

"Get back yeh foul beast. Get back!"

The large Martian Smeargoshen snorted loudly out of its six snouts and blew purple mucus all over Measles, then ran out of the barn yelping happily.

"Blast yeh pork snouted bilge rat! Now yeh see what you've done to me uniform?"

Measles plopped down on a pile of beast feed covered in mucus and tried hard not to sob. It only bore him more insults to cry in front of the Martian troops. He searched his pocket for his handkerchief, used it to wipe the purple goo from his face and started to make his way back to his feet.

"Commander Zebdu 'ill skin me alive if I don't feed his ghastly pet."

Measles groaned and started to search again for the animal. He whistled as loudly as he could.

"Here boy! Come an' get yer supper now. Nice fresh beef stew 'ere for yeh. Come on yeh mangy beast. Come and eat yer blasted stew!"

The large animal galloped towards Measles happily and plopped down in anticipation of its supper.

"There yeh are yeh mangy beast."

The animal ate loudly and breathed heavily through all six snouts. Measles sat on a large wooden bucket used to feed the Martian beasts and took off his hat. He patted the big Martian beasts head and sighed.

"Even though yer a bit of a brute I get yeh. You're of far better spirits than these odder Martian beasts I can tell yeh that. An' yer me only friend these days so I guess I better treat yeh kind. I ain't got a friend neither 'ere nor there these days."

The cold winds of Gateway City swept through the barn. Where Measles was sitting. Measles could see the chilly night sky and Epsilon's icy light shining in the distance. The stars of the heavens didn't dare shine on Gateway City.

"Chuckles ol' boy, I do miss yeh. You must be havin' a grand ol' time flyin' high in the heavens with all them beaut' stars. Tell the rest of da boys hello fer me ol' boy."

Measles got up, gave the Smeargoshen one more pat on the head and trudged back to his tent. Epsilon had invited him to dinner that evening and had promised Measles a good time, which made him very nervous. Nonetheless, he scurried to his tent, changed for dinner and made his way to the Arc.

* * *

"Measles—there you are. We were all starting to wonder if you had gotten lost. Now that you are here we can begin. I've brought all of you here to plot out our hunt for the star scrolls. But first, Measles, I'd like to introduce you to General Madix. General Madix will be leading the clowns' search for the star scrolls and will report directly to me."

After hearing Epsilon's introduction, Measles stood frozen in the center of the room. His face turned pale, even under his white clown makeup. Measles never thought that he would lay eyes on General Madix again yet there he was; standing right in front of him. General Madix peered at Measles with a hint of disdain while he chewed on pumpkin seed shells.

"The name is Measles eh? What's yer family name?"

Measles could barely speak, and he attempted to clear his throat.

"Uh, Bloghorn sir. Me father was Goldie Bloghorn."

"Old Goldie Bloghorn eh?" General Madix laughed. "I do remember that good fer nothin' ol' bloke. He thought that he was a gift from the celestials above he did. I 'ad to teach him a thin' er two more than once. Yes, indeed I did. I hope that I won't be havin' to do the same with yeh."

"Popcorn!" General Madix yelled. "Where is that daft clown? Popcorn! There yeh are yeh jelly toaded liver mule. Fetch me another potion...now!"

A very jovial looking clown tumbled clumsily into the room. "Yes sir. My apologies sir. Right away sir."

Popcorn ran from the room; tripping over his own feet at least two times. He returned with a potion. Measles expected him to spill the potion because of his erratic movements, but—despite his jitters—the happy clown never did.

"Don't linger about. Be gone with yeh." General Madix barked angrily.

Popcorn looked disappointed to be dismissed so soon, but he did as he was told and sluggishly retreated to the back of the room.

"Now then, let's begin. Many myths have risen over the years about the star scrolls. You may have heard of the scroll of Felanthiam, Rigil, and Arev, but there are thirteen scrolls that were written with the power to control space, time and all living energy. We must find the other twelve star scrolls; the six scrolls that were born of light and the six that were born of darkness. The thirteenth scroll is what binds them all together. The deylai will handle the scrolls of darkness. They will need to journey to the other heavens and the great beyond to have an audience with the dark forces. You clowns will search for the scrolls of light. I have the scroll of the Trolls of Alniyah in my possession, which we can use to help find the other dark scrolls.

"What are yeh plannin' on doin' with all o' them scrolls, Epsilon?"

"The scrolls, Measles, hold the power of life and death in space and time as we know it. They reveal the mysteries of the celestials in the highest heavens and every being and magical form in the universe. Each scroll was infused with the magic of that realm and, when mixed with enchantments and read aloud, the one that has the power of all thirteen scrolls can rule with the power of all of the thirteen forms of magic combined. With this power, I will be the morning and the evening star. I will make my return to the heavens and rule the galaxies from on high. All will bow to me and I will only shine upon those that are worthy. Those that are found unworthy will live in darkness. I can feel my power growing just from the Alniyan scroll. I need the other magical forms to complete the chain and then the thirteenth magical form to bond it."

General Madix's gray eyes lit up with a content and eerie glow at the sound of Epsilon's words. Some said that he was the oldest clown alive and that dark magic kept his heart beating for centuries past his time. Measles tried not to look at him but couldn't look away. General Madix was there the day Measles mother learned the news that his father had died. Measles remembered the General's solemn, dead gaze as he stood silently in the corner of his childhood home. His dad's war buddy Bluth and his son Popcorn came over every day after that to check on them until Measles joined the royal clown brigade. *Popcorn, Huh? I wonder if he be the same lad I used to play with as a boy?* He thought. Epsilon's sharp voice brought Measles back to the conversation.

"This clown militia is to be kept secret. No one must know- no one. If word gets out, you will all pay for your recklessness with your lives clowns. Measles, you and Popcorn will travel with General Madix through the gateway to find Proxima Centauri. He is the last celestial Prince of the lost Arokayan universe and the only royal star left of his line to guard the Arokayan Scroll of the Centauries."

Measles' head started to spin. All he wanted to do was go home, and now he was about to be sent on a journey that would lead him even further from it. He sipped his blue drink and tried not to tremble.

"Brilliant plan, Epsilon. Me boys an' I are ready to leave at first light."

"I wish that could be, Madix. Unfortunately, the celestials have found my gateway to the heavens and have been launching attacks on Mars. It's not safe to travel there now. Once we push back their forces, you can all go through. Be ready to travel at a moment's notice from this time on. Measles, leave us. I need to speak to Madix alone."

"Take that slow-witted clown with yeh an' fit him to his new quarters," growled General Madix.

Once the clowns exited the room, Epsilon turned to General Madix.

"You've served me faithfully for a long time now Madix, and in return I've asked the dark Lord Ranis to grant you long-life. You've lived the life you were given in servitude to me. I wish there were more clowns such as you."

"It 'as been me honor great one."

"I had a vision Madix. I saw Measles in Pearl City, but his path is not clear to me. I've just received news that Duchess and the fairy General have escaped. They will come here to travel to Eucharon, and when they arrive, you and your clowns will do exactly as I say."

* * *

Measles was happy to be excused, since his stomach was starting to growl very loudly. *I figured me was invited to dine with Epsilon?* He thought. *I guess I'll 'ave to scrape up me own din'.* Popcorn finally caught up to Measles after the clowns had been excused.

"Well 'ello there pal, how yeh be? Me name is Popcorn, yeh see. I'm glad to acquaint yeh this fine night, an' dine with anoder fine clown with such an' appetite."

Popcorn laughed heartily at his witty rhyme.

"Oh my. I only be jokin'. Yeh sees, I used to be in King Clownington's Royal Jestership before we was all drafted into the army. I come from a long line of jesters, yeh see. Me ma was in the Royal Jestership, an' me grand old da' before her, an' me great grandma before him an'..."

"I think I get yer drift ol' boy," Measles said with a bit of a grin.

"There's that old clown grin! Golly I'd never seen such gloomy clowns as I seen 'ere. I'm up to the challenge, I tell yeh. Me ma used to say that a chuckle or a grin, can make the dark seem less dim."

"I hope that's true, friend. I do hope it's true. Tell me Popcorn—does yer da' happen to be old Bluth Cobbin?"

"Well, I'll be me aunt Milly. How do yeh know me da'?"

"It's me, yeh jolly old fool! Measles Bloghorn. I can't believe in all me years that it's little Popcorn Cobbin. I still remember settin' the blasted chickens on yeh. You'd be scared half to death."

Measles laughed a very wheezy, hearty laugh that echoed in the cold night air.

"'ere we are friend. Home sweet home."

Measles was surprised to see food being lain out by deylai soldiers when he walked into his tent, and Commander Achernar standing in the tent with the soldiers.

"Due to Epsilon's creation of this secret militia, you will both be kept separate from all other clown soldiers. The only other clown allowed in this tent is General Madix."

With that, Commander Achernar promptly exited the tent. The two clowns immediately pounced on the food set before them. They ripped apart a roasted crispy duck with fried pork fat and herbed farro. Their hunger began to finally subside halfway into their mincemeat pies.

"I don't remember the last time I 'ad a decent meal 'ere. Very good, I must say. So, eh, Popcorn. How did yeh come to work for General Madix?"

"Well as yeh can imagine, I didn't turn out to be much of a foot soldier, so I was assigned to serve the officers. Not really much good at that neither, to be 'onest."

Measles lit his pipe and sat back in his creaky wooden chair.

"Me da' used to call General Madix 'The Butcher.' Rumor had it that it was because of him why me da' disappeared. Yeh know he stood there nice an' quiet the day they told me mum me da' was pushin' up daisies. Didn't bodder to utter even a peep."

3

Chewy and the Sugar Valley Hideaway

Chewy grabbed Duchess' hand while she trotted hurriedly along.

"We're nearly there Duchess. We'll all be safe soon. Mr. Twill is waiting for us in the Peppermint Grove."

The light of dawn poured over the village huts that lined Sugar Valley. Once General Sharaya, Duchess and Chewy crossed the border they slowed their pace and began to breathe a little easier. They walked through the village; Gingerbread houses lined the street that took them to the Peppermint Grove. Duchess looked around in amazement.

"Chewy, how is all of this possible? I've heard stories growing up, but I thought they were just fairytales."

The little gumdrop chuckled heartily.

"It's quite simple, really. I should let Mr. Twill tell you the story. He is quite the storyteller."

After a short walk down Gingerbread Lane, Duchess began to see peppermint-striped cottages and assumed that they had finally arrived at Peppermint Grove. Chewy led them to a small cottage with a red and white striped door. She knocked on the door lightly with her tiny fist and turned the handle right away.

"Mr. Twill we're here. I've brought Duchess and the General. Mr. Twill?"

"Yes Chewy, I'm here, I'm here. Come and sit for a moment all of you. You must all be famished. We'll get you all settled, but first sit and eat. Mrs. Twill just made some fresh scones and tea. I'll fetch you all some water."

Duchess felt like she was about to collapse. They had been running the entire night with no food and little water. She plopped down on some floor cushions, and the smell of food made her mouth water.

"Here we go, dears. Fresh scones, and Mr. Twill brought up some water," said Mrs. Twill.

Duchess hastily took the water and scone and gulped both down quickly.

"Oh mercy! You poor child. I'll fetch more food and water, and of course the tea to warm everyone up. Hold tight, my dears."

The first round of the Twills' water and food brought a little life back to Duchess. She started to notice the Twills for the first time, and now she could not look away. They were medium-sized creatures with two large eyes that waved back and forth on two long tentacles that stood straight up. They had stubby legs and arms, and knobby little tails.

Mrs. Twill returned with more scones, a full pot of tea and a few sweet potato pancakes.

"This should do it. Chewy dear, here are a few sugar cubes and fudge for you, love."

Mr. Twill cleared his throat loudly.

"Now then, we have business to attend to. As the Twills say, business is best to be done before you rest. You are both safe here for the moment, but it's only a matter of time until the clowns come and search the village. They will tread carefully as long as we cooperate with them. They don't want to run the risk of anything happening to their precious sugar trade. If the deylai come, they will not show mercy to anyone here. You will all stay here for the night, and we will start our journey to Gateway City in the morning."

"You must be joking. There is no way that I will ever set foot in that horrible place. I've seen it; Epsilon's tower. I saw it when I was under his spells. I can't...I won't. I want to stay here."

"Duchess, listen to Mr. Twill. The Twills are known to be among the wisest beings on this planet. Many travel far and wide to hear their counsel. I'm sure that Mr. Twill has all of our best interests in mind. I'll make sure that nothing happens to you. I promise. Please continue Mr. Twill."

"Thank you General Sharaya."

Mr. Twill sipped his tea while he cleaned his glasses. He reached into a small chest that sat beside his chair and retrieved a scroll bound in leather. Mr. Twill cleared his throat, unrolled the scroll and began to deliver the details of his plan once more.

"Where was I? Oh yes. Everyone gather around my trusty map I have here. This map has been in the Twill family for generations and has never let any of us Twills down.

Now, we must make our way to Gateway City without being discovered. I imagine that the clowns will guard the main roads and harbors, so we'll have to make our way through the dark forest and then hike through the Ironside Mountains. That should bring us right to the Sea of Flowers. The Twills have known Halan, King of the Tanatoors for many, many years. The Cantarian Tanatoors will help us cross. They have resisted Epsilon's bribery and remain loyal to the high celestials. The deylai will not expect us to be coming to Gateway City, so I suspect we should be able to cross through Crystal Valley undetected if we are quick about it. The celestials have spies in Gateway City that will help lead us to the Eucharon passage. General, you look concerned."

"Mr. Twill. Please be assured that I mean no disrespect, but it's simply too dangerous to cross the Sea of Flowers. The deylai will be guarding that route heavily, and the Tanatoors are in the middle of a civil war. The Simeons will attack us, and we will be the cause of the largest battle since the conflict has started. If we do this, we are putting Halan and all Cantarians in jeopardy."

Mr. Twill sat very still. His three fingers tapped each other very slowly and methodically as he pondered the situation.

"Hmmm. This is quite the debacle indeed. What do you suggest that we do General?"

"We should go through the Ironside Mountains as you suggested, but we should journey all the way through the mountains and continue on to the Valley of Shadows—then go directly to

Crystal Valley from there."

"You must be mad, General! We can't risk being that close to Witch Kingdom. Have you not heard of the terrors that dwell in the Valley of Shadows? Madness. Utter and...deliberate madness it is."

"I agree with your concerns Mr. Twill, but unfortunately we do not have many options. At least any blood spilled on our journey through the Valley of Shadows will be our own."

Mr. Twill calmly reached for his tea and sipped slowly. He placed his cup steadily back onto his saucer. He continued to sit without saying anything quite longer than anyone had expected. When he finally spoke again, Duchess jumped a little out of surprise.

"Well, as we ponder our options this might be a good time to tell you all the story of how the Twills came to be. The Twills often say that, 'The best stories that are told often help our thoughts to unfold.'

My grandpapa told me that the Twills of old were born of a twinkle in Felanthiam's eye that lost its way, fell through the drop of a tear and landed on a pile of stardust. When discovered by Felanthiam—our beloved mother of all stars—she ordained the Twills to be the sacred keepers and high priests of the celestial scrolls. We Twills value wisdom above all else, and have been aids to the wise high celestials from the days of the ancient Council of Crepusculum until now. We were even there when the council split, and the celestial alliance came to power.

Grandpapa told us stories of the epic battle that King Augustus and his soldiers fought—when he drove the dark ruler Loxidor the Omnipotent and his trolls out of the universe and into the lowest heavens. Days later Loxidor broke into the celestial library and slaughtered the Twills in search of his star scroll. He captured and tortured some of us to try and force us to reveal the scrolls' location, but the Twills are strong, you see. We did not break. Felanthiam carried us to a very special hidden place on earth called Normandeery, where we've lived in peaceful seclusion for centuries. Every Twill is taught a prayer to say at night before we sleep.

May our eyes close and wake in peace, and may harm and darkness never find us. For we are the sacred keepers of the light, and the heavens will always guide us.

The Twills of Normandeery grew larger and larger in number, and lived long lives hidden in the hills. At a ripe old age, each Twill returns to the twinkle of the stars' eyes. One day Loxidor will find us, which is why we have to make it to Gateway City. I must speak to the celestial alliance and beg for their help..."

There was a brief moment's pause, and then Mr. Twill said, "Well now, look at all of these mopey faces! Cheer up. I've just figured out our route to Gateway City. I suggest, General, that we strike a compromise. We shall journey through the Ironside Mountains since we both agree that's best. I think that we should still take the passage through the Sea of Flowers, but we shall stick to the shallow regions. The Tanatoors stay in the deeper regions, so we will not alert Halan of our presence. What do you say, General?"

"With all due respect Mr. Twill, I can't say that it's the most brilliant plan I've ever heard—or necessarily a compromise—but we have to get to Gateway City somehow. If something alters our plans, we must be prepared to face the possibility of going through the Valley of Shadows."

"I couldn't agree with you more, General. Thank you for being so amiable. Well, now that we've decided that, I think that we should all get some rest. I'll say, 'Goodnight,' now. 'Rest is always best,' as the Twills say."

* * *

Duchess tossed and turned on her mat filled with straw. It was a comfortable and cozy bed, even though is was on the floor. Mrs. Twill had warmed heavy cotton sheets and warm blankets for Duchess and General Sharaya to sleep on. She rolled over and caught a glimpse of Chewy standing guard. The tiny gummy figure walked back and forth with a rather severe expression. Chewy peeked at Duchess and noticed she was awake.

"Duchess are you ok? Should I fetch the General?"

"No...no thank you Chewy. I'm sure I'll fall asleep soon."

"I can ask Mrs. Twill to make you some warm milk.?"

"Oh no, thank you Chewy. I just seem to have such terrible dreams when I close my eyes. I may just step outside for some fresh air."

"I don't think that's such a good idea Duch..."

"I feel like I can't breathe in here. I need just a little air. I'll put my hood on so that no one recognizes me."

Duchess stepped outside into the cool night and felt the light breeze on her face. She listened to the sound of the wind with her eyes shut tight and heard the faint voices of creatures singing.

"Chewy, do you hear that? Who is singing that lovely tune?"

"Oh, it must be the marshmallow miners. They love to mine the sugar caves at night. The sun is too hot for them during the day."

"This place is more magical than Clown Town. Was Sugar Valley created by the celestials as well?"

"We all came to be by rather dark magic that was cast upon us long ago by the celestial sorceress that used to live on high, Vangemtra. We were for the pleasure of the witches and warlocks. The fairies took us in and created this place for us during the old war. The clowns treat us fair enough, and practically live off of our sugar supply."

"Oh Chewy, I wish I could stay here. It's such a long way to Eucharon and the road to Gateway City is dangerous."

"Don't you worry about a thing, Princess. I'll be beside you the whole way. I promise. Now hurry along now. You must get back inside."

Duchess wandered wearily back into the cottage and crawled back onto her small cot. Her mind raced with everything that had already happened. She still felt that her strength had not returned since she was under the spell of the Conjurer. *Princess? Why would Chewy call me a princess? Oh mom, I wish you were here. I have so many questions.*

4

The Celebration of Night

"Darkness is rather an' odd thing don't yeh think now, Popcorn? After bein' 'ere in Gateway City fer so long I can't even really remember the sun. Ain't that the oddest thing?"

"Oh I remember the sun, ol' chap. It's like that warm flush that hits yeh when yeh open a warm oven to pull out a fresh loaf a' bread. It warms yer very soul. It weren't too long ago that I was walkin' down Main Street in Clown Town, feelin' the bright sun on me eyelids."

"Aye. Was long ago fer me, Pop."

Measles felt a tingle in his nose.

"Ah...ah...ah...achooey!"

"Gesundheit! You still 'ave that nasty cold eh?"

"Can't seem to shake it, Pop. It's a cold that goes deep to me bones I tell yeh. Eeeyow!" Measles yelped.

"Take it easy, Meas. Yeh don't have to do all the liftin' yerself now. I'll give yeh a hand, friend."

"Pop, yer sent straight from the stars I swears. I don't know what I'd do without yeh 'ere I tell yeh."

"Alright now Meas, alright. Let's get these piles a wood to the fire pits before General Madix filets our hides."

Measles grunted while he pulled the large piles of wood into one of the fire pits that surrounded Gateway City.

"How many...how many more fire pits we got left Pop?" Measles wheezed.

"Well let's see 'ere. Looks like we just did uh one... two...two. We did two, so now we got to do uh 1,2, 3,4,5,6,7,8,9,10,11 more. See Meas, we're almost done!"

"Almost done? They're thirteen of these pig-snouted fire holes? Argh!" Measles groaned.

"Are yeh sure Epsilon wanted 'em all filled with wood an' kindle?"

"General Madix was extremely forthright. He practically put his hands around me neck an' told me that the thirteen flames are vital to the celebration of night an' not to screw it up."

"Alright, alright. What we got to do after fillin' the skunk-livered fire pits?"

"Looks like we also gotta setup these 'ere, uh. I don't even know what these be. What do yeh think these are, Meas?"

"Looks like a table of some sort. Would be my guess anyways."

"I guess it's no stranger than anything else goin' on 'ere.

Alright Meas, we best get a move on. Let's make it a game and see how fast we can fill these 'ere pits, eh? I'll race yeh to the next one!"

The clowns both whooped and hollered as they slapped the hides of their Martian beasts and raced to the next fire pit on the edge of Gateway City.

* * *

Measles and Popcorn put the Martian beasts back in their pens and began to walk wearily back to their tent, but they seemed to be walking in the opposite direction of everyone else. Measles spotted Martian Commander Zebdu out of the corner of his eye walking right towards them.

"Quick Pop, let's go this way. Look who's comin'."

"Where do you clowns think you're going?" Roared Commander Zebdu.

"Please Commander, we don't want no trouble, sir. We be famished an' been working quite a while now, sir."

A grin crossed the face of the Martian Commander.

"Do not worry, clowns. We will all feast on flesh tonight, and you both will be my guests of honor."

Commander Zebdu took both clowns by the collar and dragged them along with him and his men to the center of the city.

Measles and Popcorn began to shake at the sound of chanting from the Martians, and dark stars gathered there. The Martians were dancing around the biggest fire pit that was in the center of the city, and Measles remembered how long it took him and Popcorn to fill that particular fire pit with wood and kindle. Commander Zebdu threw the clowns on the ground near the pit and he and his men began to chant and dance around the clowns. Measles and Popcorn crouched down and covered their ears at the sudden sound of shrieking laughter that poured into the dark sky. Those that gathered around the fire pits cheered loudly.

"What a celebration this will be!" Commander Zebdu exclaimed.

The Commander grabbed the necks of both clowns that were now trembling in fear and forced them to their feet.

"Stand you cowards in the presence of greatness. Even the Martians stand in awe of the power of the witches, and they have gathered here with us to celebrate the night."

The witches touched down by each of the thirteen fire pits and conjured large black caldrons filled with bubbling potions. The armies of the dark stars and Martians ran to them, and the witches filled the soldiers' mouths with black liquid from the caldrons. A cold wind began to blow, and the clowns looked again to the sky and saw Epsilon ascend high into the dark heavens above Gateway City. Epsilon flew over the piles of wood and kindle for the thirteen fires and lit them. His voice echoed through the entire camp as he spoke.

"To all that have come, hear my voice. We have gathered here to honor the dark forces of the lower heavens and remember the fallen, but we must know where we began in order to lead this realm into our new era of dark magic. My children remember where we have come from!"

Epsilon waved his hand and a map of the thirteen realms appeared in the air that surrounded the soldiers. Epsilon gazed upon his creation with delight and began to speak again to the warriors that gathered there.

"The thirteen heavens are shaped like a cylinder. The heavens of light dwell in the upper heavens, and the kingdoms of the dark in the lower heavens. Tonight we light thirteen flames and offer thirteen souls of our enemies to honor the fallen and the dark Lords of the galaxies of the eternal dark. We will one day unite the thirteen scrolls, and we will not stop fighting until we have them all. Those of us who have been cast out of the heavens will look down upon those who are now on high; crawl lifelessly on desolate planets. Each of you has gathered around an altar, bring forth your sacrifice and let us feast!"

Commander Zebdu and his men roared in harmony with the thirteen legions that had gathered. The Martian army chanted in unison and gathered around their Commander, dancing wildly.

"Martians, we gather here to honor Aima, the God of Moons, who gives us our strength to tear flesh from bone. To you Aima, here is our offering!"

Commander Zebdu grabbed Measles and Popcorn and threw them on the altar. The Martians cheered and danced with more passion than before around the two clowns that laid helplessly awaiting their doom.

"I never thought this would be me end, Pop," Measles sobbed.

"We never be nothin' more than food to these creatures. What we even be doin' 'ere with 'em? I never knew the clowns to be so powerless in all me years, but indeed we be nothin' to 'em an' we'll soon be ground meat."

"Don't cry now, Meas. We're not goners yet. It takes a bit

of time for the wood to catch fire. Once the fire is lit we jump, yeh hear me? Everyone is busy drinkin' an' dancin' they won't see us."

"They'll find us, Pop. They'll find us an' gut us like fish, I tell yeh."

"We'll 'ave to hide out fer a few days an' find General Madix, but we'll make it, Meas. Don't yeh worry now. We'll make it."

The clowns laid waiting and watching the Martians dance with torches of fire in their hands. Commander Zebdu yelled a command in some Martian language that the clowns could not understand, and the Martian soldiers threw their torches onto the altar.

"Not yet, Meas. Stay calm an' in the center. Wait fer da smoke to grow a bit," Popcorn ordered.

Measles felt his clown makeup start to drip from his face because of the heat. The two clowns crouched down and tried to shield their faces from the smoke that was building.

"Now Measles, now!" Popcorn ordered.

The two clowns used all of the strength that they had to jump from the altar and they landed right beside the wall of the city.

"Measles...you ok, Measles?"

Measles patted the small flame that was burning on his pant leg and tried his best to catch his breath.

"I think I still be livin'. You alright, Pop?"

"I think we both made it, Meas."

"What do we do now, Pop? Eeyow!"

"Measles? Measles? What happened? I can't see nothin'."

Popcorn squinted his eyes and saw something glimmer in the light of the flames burning all around them before he felt a bag pulled over his head.

"Is that...is that a gumdrop?"

* * *

Epsilon gazed upon the celebration with pride from on high in his dark tower. The smoke from burning flesh and wood wafted through the room. The scent reminded him of his days spent on Alniyah as a young star, learning the dark arts from his father, Mancai. The orb that opened the gateway to the heavens appeared, and Epsilon turned to see King Raka emerge from the black cloud that surrounded it.

"Raka, Ena Ga. I was worried that you would not make it to the celebration."

"Thank you, Epsilon. I came to celebrate in unison with you and your soldiers and congratulate you on your victory against the high celestials in the Martian battles. Your strength has brought us all great victory. I also have a gift for you. The Eobans attacked the temple of Aima in our rival tribal capital in the storm lands, and found the lost Martian scroll of the ancient Eobans."

"Raka, you bring me great pleasure. Great pleasure."

"The pleasure is mine, great one. You seem to be in rather pleasant spirits due to the celebration Epsilon. Shall we...what do the humans call it uh... toast? Yes, toast. Shall we toast your victory tonight?"

"By all means yes, Raka. Tonight's celebration has restored my visions. I saw something spectacular after the sacrifices were completed. Victory is coming to me as we speak."

5

The Valley of the Shadow of Death

"Can we please sing a different song, Chewy?" Duchess groaned in desperation.

"Come, come Duchess. Don't be such a gloomy Gus. Sing away your gloom, or you will surely meet your doom."

"As the Twills say, Mr. Twill?" General Sharaya said with a slight grin.

"Why of course, General," Mr. Twill said with a huff. "We Twills can make even the most humbug of creatures smile."

Chewy skipped along the rocky path and burst into song

yet again.

"Diddley dee, diddley do. I just love, a walkin' with you. Diddley dum, diddley do. Walking is my favorite thing to do!"

Duchess and General Sharaya started to lag slightly behind Mr. Twill and the singing gumdrop.

"Have you ever seen such a cheerful little creature in all your life, Duchess?"

General Sharaya couldn't help but to chuckle at the look of annoyance on Duchess' face.

"I have never in my life," Duchess said sharply.

"I'm really not sure why Chewy was chosen to come with us. How is she going to protect any of us from danger? Ouch! I have a rock in my shoe."

Duchess pouted, removed her shoe and looked for what was stabbing her toes.

"Another rock in your shoe? We must keep up, Duchess. We cannot stop until nightfall. We have to make it to the Ironside Mountains by tonight. In fact, I need to tell Mr. Twill that we should increase our pace somehow. As much as I admire Chewy's...positive attitude, this is not an afternoon stroll through the meadow. The deylai will soon be upon us."

General Sharaya ran ahead to speak to Mr. Twill.

"Alright General if we have no choice we will move faster. We Twills have top-notch athletic ability. If we have to run until nightfall, I can keep up. A Twill never disappoints."

"I never doubted you for a moment Mr. Twill. Duchess, keep up. You cannot stray from the group."

Duchess tried hard not to cry. Trekking over branches and rocks hurt her aching feet terribly.

"Poor Duchess, maybe it would help if you pretended that you were going to fly away at any moment. Yes, that's it! Your wings! You both could fly and carry Mr. Twill and me! We would get to the Ironside Mountains in no time at all that way."

"That's out of the question, Chewy. We would surely be spotted by deylai if we flew, and Duchess has never learned how to use her magic."

"I have no magic and even if I did I...I wouldn't use it ever! Only people like Epsilon and his conjurers use magic. General, since you seem to know so much about me, when will you tell me just who I am and...and where I've come from? What has happened to my family? Are they meeting us in Pearl City? Who will get them there? Chewy called me princess and I..."

"Yes, there are many questions to be answered, Duchess, but we need to focus on the journey ahead. All will be answered once we arrive safely to Pearl City. Everyone, we must move faster and reach the Ironside Mountains by nightfall. NOW MOVE. That's an order!"

Duchess did her best to keep up and was surprised that she struggled to stay close to both Chewy and Mr. Twill. General Sharaya slowed her pace and jogged beside Duchess.

"For such...for such small creatures...they...they move quite fast."

"I bet that you're regretting all of those trips to cake cottage. Just wait until we get to Pearl City, Duchess. You'll love it there. The flowers grow as tall as you and me. The water is clear, and the sun brings warmth to all that live there. You think that the cakes in Clown Town are good, wait until you taste the garsberry streusel that our Fairish chefs cook up!"

The day seemed to never end. The travelers walked and ran for hours to try and reach the Ironside Mountains by sunset.

"We made it and just in time!"

General Sharaya breathed deeply and wiped the sweat from her brow. A satisfied grin was firmly planted on her face.

"Let's set up camp here and we will all take turns keeping a lookout for deylai and clown soldiers. The next few days will be long and hard since we'll be hiking through the mountains. Try and get as much sleep as you can. If you see or hear anything suspicious use this call. Tu la loo, tu la loo."

Duchess, Chewy and Mr. Twill all sprang into action and began to set up camp for the night.

1...2...3...4. Oh, fiddlesticks. 1...2...3...4...5. I don't know why I bother to even try and sleep. I never seem to be able to. I used to be able to lay on a grassy hill in the Garden Gate Village and count the stars until I fell asleep. I guess those days are far behind me now. Duchess thought to herself.

She rolled onto her side and tried to shut her eyes once more. She pictured the starry sky in the Garden Gate Village in her mind and counted the stars that were now so far away. *1...2...3...4...5.*

"Tu la loo, tu la loo."

Mr. Twill quickly jumped to his feet.

"Chewy, Duchess, did you hear that? Was that from the General?"

Mr. Twill, Chewy, and Duchess stood in silence listening hard to the wind that blew across the Ironside Mountains that night.

"Tu la loo, tu la loo."

"Yes! It's General Sharaya. What in heaven's name do we do?" said Duchess.

The sound of someone running towards them grew louder and louder until General Sharaya burst through the trees.

"We must leave now! Grab your packs and sleeping mats, and follow me quickly. No time to waste. The deylai have found us."

Mr. Twill, Chewy, Duchess and General Sharaya quickly rolled their sleeping mats, attached them to their packs and set off through the dark mountains.

"Head into the trees!" Commanded General Sharaya. "The star flyers will not be able to spot us from there."

The tired travelers quickly veered from the path and headed into the thick trees.

"How...long...must we run General?" Duchess huffed and tried hard to steady her breath.

"Until we are safe. The deylai will touch down soon and start to hunt for us on foot. They expect us to be hiding near Clown Town instead of heading towards Gateway City. Hopefully, their pursuit will be short if they don't spot us."

The sound of the star flyers in the dark sky was enough motivation for Duchess to keep running. General Sharaya, Duchess, Chewy and Mr. Twill ran until the sun began to break through the night sky. General Sharaya huddled them all together and ordered them to crouch low while she scouted the area. Duchess felt like Sharaya had been gone for hours when she suddenly reappeared. She wasn't smiling but seemed to have a slightly more pleasant expression.

"Well, the deylai have let up for now. They are probably not used to the sunlight and may have trouble moving around during the day. We'll make camp here and move out at nightfall."

"I'll take the first watch, General. We Twills do not need as much sleep as you fairies do."

"I'll keep you company, Mr. Twill," Chewy piped in cheerfully.

"Will you please teach me the nursery rhyme that you promised me?"

"Now is not the time for all of that silliness, Chewy."

"I beg to differ, Mr. Twill. I think now is the perfect time for a bit of silliness," General Sharaya said with a slightly playful yet stern tone.

"Just keep your voices low."

"Oh, alright then. If the General insists, that is. Come on now. Let's set up watch over here."

Duchess and General Sharaya laid out their sleeping mats and crawled under their rough burlap blankets. Duchess peaked out of her blanket and saw Chewy and Mr. Twill settling into a tree to keep watch.

"Alright now, Chewy. If I remember correctly I promised to teach you one of the Twills' famous nursery rhymes, is that correct?"

"Yes. That's the one Mr. Twill, that's the one!"

"What a rhyme this one is, Chewy. Every Twill is taught this as a child. Let's see if I can remember how it goes...

Fuddly Duddly, was far from cuddly.
He was a prickly pear that didn't care,

and attended the town fair in his long underwear!

*At the fair, he dare to bring a pair
of sour rye pies, which made all the children cry.
So he played his flute and made a toot because the pie had
too much sour milk rye.
The children laughed and sang and danced, until he bid
them all goodbye.*

*He took his pie to a well that was dry and made them fly off
the edge of the well,
which seemed to quell the awful smell
of the sour rye pies that made them cry."*

Duchess was rather surprised by the pleasantness of Mr. Twill's voice. Her eyelids immediately felt heavy, and when she opened them again it was late in the day. She rolled onto her back and did her best to stretch her aching limbs.

"Look, look everyone. Duchess is awake!"

"Alright now, Chewy. We can all see this with our own eyes," Mr. Twill said dryly.

General Sharaya and Mr. Twill were sitting around a fire, and General Sharaya poured some chicken broth in a cup and walked over to Duchess.

"How did you sleep, Duchess? I haven't seen you sleep through the night in quite some time."

"I slept very well, thank you General. There must have been some magic in Mr. Twill's rhyme."

"Please, call me Sharaya. I guess that's more appropriate

considering..."

"Considering? Considering what, General?"

"Considering that technically we are related. Cousin Sharaya is really what you should call me."

Duchess was stunned at the news, and was still getting used to the never-ending surprises that occurred since she first arrived at Clown Town.

"I can't believe it! Why would my mother hide all of this from me?"

"Don't blame her, Duchess. When the Fairish portal to Eucharon was discovered by Epsilon, there were still many members of the royal Faree family that could not escape. The villagers took them in and hid them. Years passed, and Epsilon's power only continued to grow. War broke out in the heavens, and there was no safe way to get the rest of the royal family to Eucharon.

King Zionous and General Ferran have been building Pearl City and fighting alongside the high celestials. Now we have no choice. We have to get all of you out. Heaven help us, but we're finally going home, Duchess."

Duchess didn't know what to say. She wanted to cry and laugh all at the same time.

"Please, General...I mean Sharaya. Please tell me more about me...us...our family."

"All in due time. King Zionous wants to tell you the story himself. I wouldn't dare do it for him. Now then, Mr. Twill and Chewy, gather around. I think that we should travel at night and lay low during the day until we reach Gateway City. Get as much rest as you can and we'll head out again at nightfall. We will each take turns scouting the area to make sure we are not being followed by the deylai. I'll teach you all what to look and listen for on your scouting trips. We should reach the Sea of Flowers in two weeks time."

* * *

General Sharaya wiped the small speck of blood from her cheek. The steep, narrow trails of the mountains were covered with sharp rocks and thorn-covered branches that jutted into the path, mercilessly scratching the faces and bodies of the tired travelers. Even General Sharaya started to show signs of exhaustion. As the day started to break, the travelers sat around yet another campfire and ate bread and chicken broth with some fresh mushrooms that they found along the way.

"Everyone, I have good news! I think that this will be our final day spent sleeping in the mountains. I climbed up onto Avery rock this morning, and I could see the Sea of Flowers. We should be able to make it there by tomorrow morning."

"Yes, you are correct Mr. Twill, but it also looks like the clown militia has set up a port there. We will not be able to sneak past them. We must journey through the Valley of Shadows and make our way to Crystal Valley through there."

"General, we cannot journey through the Valley of Shadows. We'd be safer walking right into the clown militia camp, to be quite frank. You know better than anyone here the danger that lives in the valley. We must think of another way."

"I ca...ca...ca...can't do it. I just can't."

Chewy began to tremble.

"They say that she is there waiting to harvest 10,000 souls.

That is the price that she must pay to Ranis to return to her body. She is in the wind there, in the water, in the earth..."

Duchess stood and helplessly watched the little gumdrop burst into tears.

"Sharaya, there must be another way. I've never seen Chewy so petrified. And who is 'She?'"

Chewy was sobbing so uncontrollably that she could not answer.

"Chewy is talking about the ancient supreme sorceress Vangemtra that haunts the valley. Only a piece of her soul passed on to Lyanthra. When she gave her blood to seal the thirteenth scroll, the dark Lord Ranis allowed her the gift of life only if she gave him 10,000 souls in return. Her and her creatures haunt the valley and kill any travelers that pass through it."

"General Sharaya, I have been against going through the valley since we discussed our route in Sugar Valley. How do you propose we get through the Valley of Shadows without our souls being harvested?"

"Well Mr. Twill, it won't be easy—nor will it be safe. All that I know is that the spirits and shadows of death are not permitted to leave the valley. We must travel through the valley as quickly and silently as possible."

"This doesn't sound like much of a plan, General, but it seems that we have no other choice. Duchess, Chewy, make sure to get some rest—for we depart at nightfall."

* * *

Duchess, Chewy, General Sharaya, and Mr. Twill stood at the edge of the Valley of Shadows to soak up the last bit of sunlight that they would see until they reached Pearl City. Darkness would surround them as they journeyed through the Valley of Shadows, Crystal Valley and then finally Gateway City.

"We mustn't linger any longer now. Be silent as the grave until we reach Pearl City. Only talk if necessary and keep your voices low. You will hear the dead spirits talking to each other. Don't be frightened. Keep moving forward. Our enemies surround us, but Felanthiam will protect us."

With that said, General Sharaya illuminated her wand with a dim light and began to lead them into the valley.

After walking for what seemed like hours, Duchess felt a small hand grab hers and heard Chewy's faint sniffles. She grasped her little hand tightly as they walked along. Duchess had never encountered darkness such as this. Her eyes were open wide, yet she still couldn't see. Dark voices and screams that were carried by the wind swirled over their heads.

"How long, Mekayel? How long until Ranis frees us? I cannot bear to restlessly roam through this desolate valley anymore. I long to chant over the caldrons in the great hall of Witch Kingdom."

"Soon, sister, very soon we shall live and walk the earth. I feel stronger with every soul that I consume. When our Queen is free, we shall also be free."

"Who would dare to walk this valley and face us? Send the shadow to search far and wide and draw souls to us."

"Yes sister. I will summon the shadow of death to lure lost souls to us, so that we may harvest them for the dark Lord."

The dead spirits of the ancient witch rulers cackled loudly and began to sing and chant the spell to summon the shadow of death.

General Sharaya stopped, crouched low and gathered Duchess, Chewy and Mr. Twill around her tightly.

"The spirits are restless," she whispered. "Wait here until they pass through this part of the valley. They must sense our presence here."

Duchess shut her eyes and buried her head in her knees. The darkness of the valley suddenly deepened, and the wind grew stronger. A cold frost began to cover the valley, and the travelers could feel a dark presence sweep over them.

"I see you, fairy. Show yourself to me and your death will be painless."

"Stay low," General Sharaya commanded. "I must face him alone, and whatever happens keep going. Mr. Twill will show you the way to Gateway City if he must. Now go!"

Despite Duchess' protest, Mr. Twill pulled her and Chewy along and left General Sharaya to face the dark shadow alone.

"How dare you speak to me, shadow? I am the General of the Fairish legions. I flew with King Zionous through the darkest part of the twelfth heaven, and formed the seal that keeps the dark Lord Ranis imprisoned on Lyanthra. Even though I walk through the valley of the shadow of death, I shall fear no evil!"

The light of General Sharaya's wand grew brighter and brighter until it pierced the darkness. The shadow screamed and the cold frost of death swirled around her like a cyclone. General Sharaya raised both hands and closed her eyes. She used her magic to push against the winds of dark shadow and spoke the great Fairish words of victory, kayacum no ai. The shadow of death roared in agony until it finally retreated back into the dark sky. General Sharaya breathed heavily and immediately shot through the darkness, catching up to Duchess, Mr. Twill and Chewy.

"We have to run, now! The spirits will be here soon. They know we're here now."

The travelers set off through the dark valley at a furious pace and ran until the darkness lifted slightly. They stopped and rested for a few hours, then set off again at a slower pace. The dead spirits that haunted the Valley of Shadows flew over their heads trying desperately to harvest the souls that they felt were near. Duchess tried not to listen to the chatter of the spirits, but the sound of their dark voices began to wear on her.

"We've angered them. They are searching for us but cannot find us. How come they can't see us, Sharaya?"

"Felanthiam protects us, but we must hurry."

The souls continued to screech in anguish, and wailed loudly while they journeyed through the valley.

"General Sharaya, we must stop and get some sleep or I fear we may not make it out of the valley."

"Alright, Mr. Twill. Let's set up camp here and try to sleep for an hour or two. Everyone, wrap your blankets around your ears. It will help to drown out the voices of the dead spirits."

Duchess, Chewy and Mr. Twill covered their ears with their blankets and tried hard to block out the noise. No matter how hard Duchess pressed her hands over her ears, she could not drown out the haunting voices. She curled into a tight ball on her sleeping mat and finally managed to fall asleep.

"Oh sister, she will torture us for eternity if we do not find them."

"Don't worry Meykayel. She is coming herself to find them. We will have them tonight."

Duchess felt herself being pulled to her feet and dragged along by General Sharaya.

"General I can't..."

"Shh! We must! Vangemtra is coming for us. We must get out of the Valley of Shadows tonight. Now run, and everyone hold onto each other."

As they ran the voices of the spirits seemed to grow fainter.

"Can we please slow down now, Sharaya? I can barely hear their voices now."

"I do agree with Duchess, General. I don't know how much longer I can go at this pace."

"Alright, Mr. Twill. Let's stop and rest."

Duchess breathed a sigh of relief.

"I can barely hear the spirits any more. Thank heavens."

"I am more concerned that they have just given up all of a sudden. Who would command them to stop? Only an evil greater than Vangemtra would be able to command them to do so." Said General Sharaya.

"Everyone, put on your cold weather garments. I can see the frost on the ground, which means that we've finally reached the Crystal Valley."

6

Escape to Pearl City - Part 1

After just the first step that Duchess took out of the Valley of Shadows, she began to breathe easier. The entrance to Crystal Valley was shrouded with large crystals that jutted through the frozen ground and shot high above their heads. Even though there was still no sun, the weary travelers were all relieved to be free of the haunted voices that lived in the Valley of Shadows.

"I don't know what makes me happier at this point–being able to make a proper camp tonight, or not being followed by the ghosts of dark sorcerers," Mr. Twill remarked.

"Yes, well we will certainly be able to rest here, but never forget that we are not safe here or anywhere until we get to Pearl City. In fact, we are in more danger here than we were in the valley. Day by day we draw closer to Epsilon, and we are now in danger of being found at any moment. As for tonight, we'll make an igloo out of packed snow. It will keep us warm and hide the light of the campfire."

Mr. Twill was the first to spring into action and execute General Sharaya's orders. They each dug into the snow and began to build their icy fortress. Once they were done, they all took out their sleeping mats while Mr. Twill made the fire and started a pot of stew. Duchess took a deep breath, settled onto her sleeping mat and wrapped herself in the wool blanket that Mrs. Twill gave her for the journey. The igloo felt almost as good as her fluffy, king-size bed did back in Clown Town. Of course, this was all in comparison to having to sleep sitting up in the Valley of Shadows.

Duchess dozed off, but her eyes flickered open to the sweet smell of fresh fish stew. Duchess sleepily rolled off of her mat and sat by the fire.

"Do I smell fish stew?"

"Why yes! Mr. Twill is quite the genius when it comes to ice fishing."

Chewy grinned happily while sitting comfortably on a stump made of snow.

"Well, I am truly humbled, Chewy. Thank you for the compliment. I used to go ice fishing with my grandfather on Murathim a very, very long time ago. We Twills don't mind the cold. We're built for hostile weather conditions. I do wish I would have remembered to ask Mrs. Twill to pack some of the fresh herbs that she uses for her fish stew. As the Twills say, 'When not planned, you are d...' Oh my. I can't seem to remember the rest of it. I must be in need of more sleep. Forgive me, it will come to me."

"We have no doubt Mr. Twill," Duchess chuckled. "Where is General Sharaya?"

"Stargazing," Chewy chimed in.

Duchess pulled on her wool socks, boots and cape to brave the cold. She stepped outside of the cozy little igloo, and saw General Sharaya gazing at the sky not too far away.

"What are you looking at, Sharaya?"

"Wait for it...I think it's nighttime now. Hard to tell without the sun. Look, there it is!"

"It's magnificent. I've never seen anything so beautiful!"

"Her voice is just as beautiful as the light she brings to this dark place. Her name is Aurora Borealis, and she sings at every prominent royal gathering of the celestials. I can still hear the sound of the Fairish instruments that accompany her. It's the sweetest sound that you will ever hear.

It's been far too long since I've been home, Duchess. I'm starting to forget the sound of the voices of the ones that I love. Come, let's go back inside. It's cold, and I have something to tell all of you."

The two made their way back into the igloo and sat by the fire.

"Alright, everyone. I think that we have all gotten some much-needed rest and we need to continue on once we see the light of Epsilon fade. This signals that nighttime has come. We will need to stop and see Polus first. He has been instructed to give me the scroll of High Celestial King Augustus Celenamis to take with us to Pearl City for safe keeping. It's a miracle that he has been able to hide it right under Epsilon's nose for so long. Epsilon has been trading souls for the ancient books of dark magic. This has deprived him of his visions, but it will not be for long. He will soon be able to overcome this and grow even more powerful from the knowledge he has gained from the dark texts that he's gathered so far. We have learned that he now has the ancient book of the star of Andeeri."

Mr. Twill grew somber, put down his bowl of stew and slowly wiped his mouth.

"Yes, a very dark book and a dark tale that comes with it," Mr. Twill commented. "Even the Twills that kept watch over it when it was in the high celestial library long ago went mad. Polus seemed to be unaffected by its power, and it was decided by the celestial alliance to have it brought here to earth for Polus to watch over it. When Epsilon came to power here on earth, it was his for the taking."

"What is this dark tale that you speak of?" Chewy asked with big round eyes.

"Not now, Chewy. All will be revealed in due time," Mr. Twill barked. "General please continue."

"Thank you, Mr. Twill. I was able to communicate with Aurora Borealis, and she has called for the arctic wolves to bring supplies. They have stolen sleds and uniforms used by the clowns, so if the deylai see us from above we will look like members of the Royal Clown Brigade. Mr. Twill and Chewy will have to hide under our packs during the journey. King Amarok

himself is coming with them. The arctic wolves have fought beside the fairies since the old war, and I trust King Amarok with
my life. He will do everything in his power to help us arrive safely.
We'll travel in the darkest part of the day and rely on the wolves'
night vision to guide us. We leave in a few hours, so rest up."

Duchess tried her best to keep the icy air from stinging her
face. She re-tied her scarf around her neck and pulled it over
her nose and mouth. The clown uniforms and wigs that she and
General Sharaya were now wearing were quite warm. Duchess
shut her eyes for a moment and tucked her head into her scarf.
She began to doze when General Sharaya jolted her awake.

"Duchess wake up, you can't miss this. Look! The crystals
in the valley reflect the northern lights when they are in the sky.
Aurora is watching over us."

Duchess gazed upon the pink, green, purple and blue
lights that surrounded the sled as they reflected onto the large
crystals of the valley that poked through the snow.

"It's incredible Sharaya. Just absolutely amazing."

Duchess looked in the back of the sled and saw Chewy's
and Mr. Twill's heads poking out to see the colors.

"The speed of the wolves is impeccable Sharaya. Are they
going to run all night?"

"They are truly brilliant creatures. They'll stop and rest
soon and then we'll be off again. We should reach Polus' cave by
Epsilon's light."

Duchess' eyes soon began to close again. Between the co-
ziness of the sled and the sound of the running wolves, she was
lulled gently to sleep. Her eyes fluttered slightly when she felt

the sled stop. Duchess heard General Sharaya leave the sled and speak to the lead wolf, who she assumed was King Amarok. His deep wolf voice was fierce, but it also made her feel safe at the same time. General Sharaya returned to the sled and they were off again.

"I've never seen wolves this large, Sharaya. They are quite fearsome creatures."

"Fearsome, yes, but also kind. King Amarok's line of wolves descends from an ancient line that has protected the fairies from the days of old when we lived on earth. We fairies are not only the caretakers of the stars but also all living things. We cared for the wolves, and in turn the wolves cared for us. King Amarok and I have been friends for a very long time. He was part of the council that tried to reason with Epsilon. When Epsilon built Gateway City, he convinced many of the arctic wolves to join him. Civil war still plagues them, and King Amarok and those loyal to him have gone into hiding. This is a very dangerous journey, but he and his soldiers are risking their lives to get us back to Eucharon. We forever owe them our gratitude. Look Duchess, we've made it—and just in time."

Duchess looked into the distance and noticed an eerie blue light in the distance light up the valley and a red glow from a cave that they were approaching quickly.

"The blue light is the light of Epsilon. There is Polus' cave in the distance. He will be glad to meet you," said General Sharaya.

The sled pulled to a stop in front of the cave and the wolves all stood breathing heavily from their run. King Amarok walked quietly to the sled.

"Stay here while I make sure no deylai are here."

King Amarok walked into the cave and the rest of his soldiers walked around it to ensure the perimeter was safe. After a few moments, he emerged with a steaming pot of stew in his mouth. He set the pot of stew down where his soldiers began to gather, then walked back to the sled.

"General Sharaya, It looks to be safe, but I recommend haste. Polus has graciously made us food. We will eat, then be on our way. Retrieve the scroll quickly."

"Of course, Amarok. I was thinking the same thing. You know how much he loves to share his stories. We will do our best to hurry."

With that, the four travelers emerged from the sled. Duchess never thought that she would want to use her legs again after walking so much over the past few weeks, but she was actually glad to stand after sitting for so long. Duchess, Mr. Twill and Chewy all followed General Sharaya into the cave. The pungent smell of the stew and fresh bread reminded Duchess of just how hungry she was.

"Polus. It seems that you were expecting us old friend. It's been at least half a millennia since I've had your Swordfish stew."

"Did you come all this way just to flatter an old man Sharaya?"

Polus rose from his desk and hugged the General warmly.

"Of course, Polus. How are you holding up here in the cold?"

Polus sighed deeply.

"This never-ending darkness does have an effect on the mind and body. Being surrounded by these paralyzed souls for my only company also doesn't suit me, but this is the price that I must pay. No more of that now. Come this way. I'm sure you are all cold and hungry."

The four travelers walked by the lifeless bodies that sat motionless and covered in dust and spiderwebs at a long table, and ventured deeper into the cave. A bright warm fire raged with a large pot over it. An oven carved out of rock spewed the essence of freshly baked bread. The travelers sat on the small stools that surrounded the fire, and Polus handed out large bowls of stew, plates of bread and cups of water to Mr. Twill, Duchess and General Sharaya.

"What do you eat, little one?" Polus asked Chewy.

"Just a few cubes of sugar would be nice to have, sir."

"Of course, child. Here you go, dear. Now we can all sit and eat together."

"Polus, we cannot stay," urged General Sharaya. "Amarok is beside himself already that we've taken too long as it is, I'm sure."

"Nonsense! Everyone, eat. It will only take a moment. Make sure that you bring a few loaves of bread for the wolves as well. Who knows when I will ever see another friend. To see you, dearest Duchess, brings such joy to my heart. I remember how you toddled around the palace ballroom on two wobbly legs such a long time ago. How much you've grown, child. Now Sharaya, I assume that you all plan to somehow get through Epsilon's gateway to the heavens?"

"Yes, Polus. That is the plan," General Sharaya said impatiently.

"Well the celebration of night will draw most of the troops

to the center of the camp, and Epsilon will be in his tower for sure. This seems to be in your favor, but you still have to find your way to the portal. A treacherous journey lies before you, but take hope. You will soon be home.

If you only knew how much the universe needs you all. I once heard Orion say, 'Our journey through the perils of life is like a diamond that is refined by fire. It comes out strong and resilient on the other side.'"

"Thank you, Polus. We treasure your words of wisdom. I could listen to your wise words until the end of time, but we must go."

"Yes, you are right, General. Here, take these sacks of bread to the wolves and be gone with you."

"Thank you, Polus. We will see each other again, old friend. I promise. I will speak to the celestial alliance about granting you passage to Eucharon. Where is the scroll of High Celestial King Augustus Celenamis?"

"No, my dear. This is the price I must pay for what I've done. At least I can do this one thing for you."

Polus walked over to a wall of the cave and moved a rock, which revealed a scroll. He slowly took the scroll in his hand and turned to face the General. Polus clasped both of General Sharaya's hands in his own as he handed her the scroll.

"May the stars guide you and the scroll of Augustus home in safety."

General Sharaya embraced her old friend.

"May Felanthiam shine down upon you and keep you safe as well my dear friend."

Duchess, General Sharaya and Mr. Twill rushed from the cave and back to the sled. The wolves gobbled up the bread in one big gulp almost as soon as Mr. Twill gave it to them, and they were on their way to Gateway City within seconds. After traveling for a few hours, the sled came to a stop. King Amarok took a moment to catch his breath then approached the sled to speak with General Sharaya.

"General, we dare not go any closer. You will have to walk from here."

"Of course, Amarok. I cannot express how grateful we are for your help. You've risked your lives for us and we will forever be grateful. May the heavens watch over you and soon may there be peace among your people."

"Same to you, my friend. May you travel in safety until you reach the ones you love."

The travelers grabbed their packs from the sled and the giant wolves turned and ran in the other direction. They were soon out of sight, and Duchess, General Sharaya, Mr. Twill, and Chewy gazed upon the daunting wall of Gateway City. The sound of screams from the Martian soldiers, the beating of drums and the cackle of witches filled the air. Duchess felt Chewy's small trembling hand in her own and held it tight.

"Everyone gather around," whispered General Sharaya. "Chewy and Mr. Twill should hide in our packs. Duchess, keep your head down and follow me through the gate. Hopefully, we won't be recognized in these clown brigade uniforms, but we'll need to stay close to the wall once inside. Do you understand?"

"Yes...I'll stay close to you."

"Alright. Mr. Twill and Chewy climb in and let's go."

General Sharaya began to walk briskly towards the wall, and Duchess was close on her heels. They kept their heads down and walked right past the deylai guards guarding the gate. They ran to the wall and hid behind some sort of altar with fire on top of it.

"Ok. Now everyone stay here. I need to scout the city to find out exactly where the gateway to the heavens is. I'll be back as soon as I can."

"Wait Sharaya, did you see that? It looks like two clown guards just fell into the bushes," said Duchess.

"What? Where?"

"Close to the wall right over there."

"I'll check it out stay here."

General Sharaya drew her sword and crept by the wall towards the clowns. She noticed them both rolling around in the bushes, trying to put out the small fires that burned their uniforms. The clowns both stood up and looked in her direction. She froze, and it seemed that they were looking past her. General Sharaya tried not to move and slowly looked behind her to see Chewy was outside of Duchess' pack, and was staring right at the clowns. *Why is Chewy out of Duchess' pack? Now they've spotted us!* She thought.

General Sharaya crept along the wall until she was close enough to reach the clowns. She spotted two burlap sacks laying on the ground close to them and grabbed them. She snuck behind the first clown and easily covered his head with the sack and wrestled him to the ground. She quickly bound his hands with the long vines that grew up the wall. Since the second clown stood frozen in fear without moving, General Sharaya pounced on him and wrestled him to the ground as well, then bound his hands.

"This be our end Pop. The Martians found us out. Please don't sacrifice us, commander! We done nothin' to deserve bein' sacrificed."

"Hush, clown. You'll give us all away!" General Sharaya hissed.

General Sharaya ran close enough to Duchess, Mr. Twill and Chewy to beckon them over to where she was.

"I found these two clowns and I have an idea. We will make them take us to the gateway."

"Do you think they will, Sharaya?"

"We won't give them a choice, Duchess. Help me sit them up."

Duchess and General Sharaya tugged at the clowns' collars to prop the clowns against the Gateway City wall and removed the burlap sacks from over their heads.

"Alright you clowns. I am General Sharaya of the Faree clan and Commander of the Fairish legions. You will take us to Epsilon's gateway to the stars or die here. Now get up and take off your uniform jackets and wigs. I'll untie your hands, but if you try and run you both will meet your doom."

The clowns struggled to their feet and shed their uniform jackets and wigs. General Sharaya threw two capes in the clowns' direction.

"Put these on. Duchess, tie their hands again and then both of you start walking," General Sharaya commanded.

Once Duchess had tied the clowns' hands again, Measles and Popcorn started to trudge into the city as prisoners.

"Psst, Meas," Popcorn whispered. "Do yeh even know

where the gateway is? This General will run us through if we fail."

"I think I seen it in a room in Epsilon's tower. Pop, listen to me. This could be a blessin' fer us. We could escape to Eucharon with the fairies an' beg fer mercy. I'd rather take me chances with the fairies then stay 'ere any longer."

"Quiet you clowns. No more talking. You'll draw too much attention to us. Keep moving," General Sharaya whispered.

Mr. Twill poked his head out of General Sharaya's pack.

"General, are you sure we can trust these clowns? What if they betray us?"

"If they betray us, Mr. Twill, they will surely pay the price. We will tell the deylai that they were trying to escape. Considering these clowns were on fire when we found them, makes me wonder who tried to sacrifice them."

"What if they try to cross over with us, General?"

"Then King Zionous will decide their fate, Mr. Twill."

General Sharaya and Duchess walked through Gateway City dressed as clown brigade soldiers with Chewy and Mr. Twill hidden in their packs and Measles and Popcorn disguised as their prisoners. The sound of drums and chanting continued to surround them and the city was bright with the flames from the altars. Measles and Popcorn led them into the center of the city then stopped.

"Er uh General uh Shar... Uh General, this seems to be a rather terrible plan if yeh don't mind me sayin so."

General Sharaya pulled the clowns off of the street and into a dark corner.

"I will take no more insolence from the likes of you, clown. You will do as you're told."

"Now I mean no offense, madam. Since I 'appen to be an esteemed Royal Clown Guardsmen 'ere I think I could use me influence to get us up to the gateway is all. How did yeh plan on gettin through the deylai guards an' into the tower? It won't be as easy as walkin' through the blasted front gates, that's fer sure."

"I have little patience for your antics, clown. What do you propose?"

"Give us back our uniforms and you would be our prisoners instead."

General Sharaya shoved Measles against a brick wall, drew her sword and held it to his throat.

"Do you think me stupid, clown? You would betray us in an instant!"

"Now I meant no disrespect, General. All I be sayin' is this would be the proper way to sneak into the tower. My associate Popcorn 'ere an' I be lookin' to, uh, accompany yeh fine fairies to Eucharon if yeh be willin' to speak for us to the King out of the kindness of yer heart. Considerin' we be helpin all of yeh escape that is. What do yeh say?"

"You see, Duchess, It's just like I said. These traitorous clowns are looking to leave this place. Let me ask you a question, clown. If you and your friend are of such great importance, how is it that you were both about to be sacrificed?"

"That would be a misunderstandin', General. Between ourselves and the, uh, Martians."

"Yes, a misunderstanding indeed," General Sharaya

remarked.

Mr. Twill couldn't help but to pop his head out of the pack he was hiding in.

"General, I don't particularly see any other alternative. Considering these gentleclowns were in the process of being sacrificed when we found them, it is a safe assumption that they are victims here just as we are. In my opinion, the stars have brought us together."

"I don't like this at all, but Mr. Twill is correct. We don't have many options left."

General Sharaya began to untie the clowns' hands and Duchess pulled their uniform jackets and wigs out of her pack. Duchess and General Sharaya removed their uniforms and dawned the capes that the clowns had on.

"Uh, General, you'll have to remove yer sword an' we'll need to tie both of yer hands now."

General Sharaya reluctantly removed her sword and allowed the clowns to bind her hands.

"Since we are putting our lives in your hands, I guess we should know your names?"

"I'm Measles Bloghorn and this is Popcorn Cobbin."

"As you know, I am General Sharaya, and this is my cousin, Duchess. We have a couple of stowaways in our packs that also must get to Eucharaon. You've now seen Mr. Twill and Chewy is with us as well."

Chewy popped her head out of the bag and shyly waved her small hand.

"Well, I do say that I wish we met under happier circumstances, but it is our pleasure to meet yeh all. It looks like we

all be ready to shove off then. Say yer prayers an' let's be off."
Measles said.

7

Escape to Pearl City - Part 2

The travelers and their new found companions emerged from the dark corner where they were hiding and continued on to Epsilon's tower. General Sharaya and Duchess stared at their feet with their large hoods over their heads while the clowns led them along. After walking for some time, they came to a bridge and started to cross.

"Alright, we made it to the Arc an' we comin' up to the guards now. Keep yeh heads down no matter what." Measles whispered.

"Halt. What business do you have here?" A deylai guard shouted.

"Good evening, sirs. We are bringin' these very important

prisoners to Epsilon. He be expectin' us right away."

"Stand down. We will take them from here."

"No can do, gents. Yeh sees, we are part of the secret militia that no one is supposed to, uh, know about. So we gotta be the ones to do it. We do apologize fer the inconvenience."

"Very well. You may pass. Epsilon is in his tower."

Measles and Popcorn dragged Duchess and General Sharaya quickly along and started up the stairwell. The clowns felt quite relieved that they had made it past the guards virtually unharmed until they ran right smack dab into General Madix.

"What are yeh fools doin' 'ere? Aren't yeh supposed to be at the celebration? And where in all the blasted heavens did these two prisoners come from?"

"Well sir, yeh see...uh..."

"Run Meas, run fer yer life!" Popcorn squealed.

Popcorn ran full force into General Madix and knocked him over. General Sharaya, Duchess and Measles followed close behind him.

"Guards, after 'em!" General Madix yelled. "Yeh think yeh can run from me yeh mangy fleabags? I'll get yeh, an' when I do yeh'll cry fer yeh mothers when I get through with yeh!"

"What do we do now, Measles?"

"This was yer brilliant plan, Pop! You was the one that barreled over old Madix an' got him hoppin' mad. Keep runnin'. The gateway is on the floor right under Epsilon's potions room."

Duchess screeched loudly as she felt herself fall from someone pulling her feet out from under her.

"I got yeh now!" General Madix growled.

"Help! Sharaya, help me!"

Duchess did her best to kick General Madix with her other leg, but nothing seemed to phase the angry clown. Other clown guards began to rush towards them, and two of them grabbed onto General Sharaya. Measles and Popcorn ran to Duchess' rescue.

"Quick Pop, grab her arm an' pull like yer life depended on it. Ready? 1...2...3 heave!"

General Madix lost his balance on the narrow staircase and fell backward. Measles, Popcorn and Duchess turned and started up the stairs to help General Sharaya. The two clown guards that grabbed onto the General were already howling in pain from the blows that she was able to deliver.

"Get Duchess, Mr. Twill and Chewy to the gateway now! I'll hold them off," General Sharaya yelled.

"Come on Duchess. You 'eard General's orders. We're all about to get trampled in this blasted stairwell."

Measles and Popcorn dragged Duchess up two more flights of stairs until they reached a doorway. Measles huffed and puffed heavily as he struggled to turn the doorknob.

"Bless the saints! It's open. Our luck may be lookin' up after all."

Back on the stairwell, General Sharaya did her best to hold off the clown guards. She broke the grips of the two clumsy clowns that had caught her by the wrists and sent them rolling down the stairs. General Madix flew towards her and they both went tumbling down the stairwell. With General Madix seemingly unconscious from the fall, and the other soldiers further down the stairwell, General Sharaya made a run for it and bolted up the staircase towards the doorway. She opened the door and slammed it behind her.

"Everyone, help me barricade the door!"

Duchess, Measles and Popcorn started to pull anything that they could find over to the door to seal it shut. Mr. Twill tried hard not to lose his patience with Chewy but became quite exasperated when she attempted to help him move a chair over to the door.

"Pick it up like... Chewy pay attention and grab it from the bottom like this. That's not quite right, try holding it by the arm. Never mind, never mind. Stand back and let me do it, Chewy."

"This should be enough to slow them down for now. I'm sure more guards are on their way, but hopefully this will buy us some time. Now then, let's get this gateway to the heavens open shall we?"

"I don't see anything in here, Sharaya. There are no other doors or even windows. We've failed, and now we're trapped in this room and Epsilon's men are about to capture us."

Duchess could no longer hold back her tears and began to sob uncontrollably.

General Sharaya wiped the sweat from her brow and looked at Duchess with no frustration or anger, only pity and a twinkle in her eye.

"Have a bit of faith, my dear cousin."

General Sharaya moved closer to her weeping cousin and put a hand on her shoulder.

"Faith is the evidence of what we hold in our hearts that gives us the vision of what we cannot see."

General Sharaya withdrew her wand, held her hands in the

air and closed her eyes.

"You see, I've known Epsilon for a very long time. Since I was old enough to fight in the Fairish legions, he has been practicing dark magic. We fairies have studied him, and we know him well.

I sense the portal is here and that dark magic has hidden it from our view. We shall bring it into our existence with the magic granted to the fairies by Felanthiam herself. 'Fornus, Leemaya, Salas, Melai' means 'May what is hidden be made known to those with pure hearts, and we who are the children of light.'"

The sound of rushing wind shook the room. Duchess grabbed onto Mr. Twill and Chewy tightly and ducked her head into her cape. General Sharaya stood against the wind with wand in hand and both arms raised.

"Fornus, Leemaya, Salas, Melai. Fornus, Kanara, Melath, Halay. May the darkness that shrouds this heavenly portal be lifted and may it be revealed to the children of light!"

A small cloud of dark smoke suddenly appeared in the center of the room and swirled in a ball. It grew larger, and the dark cloud began to swirl around a globe-shaped crystal that appeared in its center. The globe lit up and shades of purple, pink and yellow sunlight overtook the dark cloud until it was no more. It floated in the middle of the room and glowed brightly.

"Everyone, quickly now. We must all touch the crystal globe together in order to pass through the gateway to the heavens. Gather around the globe and stay close to one another. Our path is set by our will so we must all act as one. Set your mind on the planet of Murathim. We will be safer landing there. Epsilon wouldn't dare to return to his former prison, and he has yet to find out the location of Pearl City. I would never risk leading him to Eucharon."

Measles and Popcorn crept fearfully towards the globe, clutching each other's arms. Chewy, Mr. Twill and Duchess formed a circle with the clowns and General Sharaya.

"Wait, I don't feel the scroll in my robe. It must have fallen out during my fight with the clowns. I have to find it. If it were to fall into Epsilon's hands, the universe would be one step closer to falling under his control."

"Sharaya, you can't go back. The deylai will come for us at any moment. What will you do against an entire legion?" Duchess said.

The deylai began to break through the barricade just as Duchess predicted. Duchess grabbed onto General Sharaya's hand.

"Come on; we must go now. Our fight is not yet over. We need help Sharaya."

With that, all six of the travelers touched the globe and instantly disappeared.

* * *

Measles and Popcorn yelped helplessly while flying through space and time. They flipped upside down and spun uncontrollably through the magical portal that transported them to Murathim. Mr. Twill flew gracefully as if he had done this a million times. He saw the clowns bouncing off the sides of the portal and did his best to help them the only way he knew how.

"Measles, Popcorn, no need for all of these flips and dips, now. Suck in those stomachs and steady yourselves. Look, even Duchess and Chewy can do it. Wonderful you two, just wonderful. No, no, no. Stop bobbing about. Don't be gormless now, do it right."

General Sharaya flew with military precision and looked behind her to make sure that those in her charge were safe.

"Is everyone alright? Hang on, we're almost there! It's going to be a bumpy landing, so make sure to tuck and roll when you hit the ground."

Swirls of bright light engulfed them as they drew near the planet. The lights were so bright and shooting past them so quickly that it made the clowns very dizzy. The cold winds of the frozen world of Murathim began to break through the swirling lights until the snow-covered ground could no longer be seen. The travelers were dropped into the soft, pillow-y snow and tumbled to a comfortable stop.

Duchess heard General Sharaya calling her name, and began to sit up and dust the snow from her face and hair. She looked around and could see a large belly and a purple and yellow striped tie sticking out of the snow. Duchess suddenly had a flashback to the clown that tried to break into her room long ago in the Garden Gate Village. The image of the oversized striped tie and large body trying to break into her cottage made her feel frightened. *No, it can't be. Could this be the same clown that tried to kidnap me?* She thought.

Duchess dismissed the thought for the present moment and looked around for the rest of her group. She saw General Sharaya and two small figures in the distance and made her way to where they were standing.

"There you are, Duchess. So glad to see we all made it in one piece. Have you spotted the clowns yet?"

"I believe they are back over there where I landed. Sharaya, I think that the large clown may be the one who..."

"Duchess, look. The celestials and members of the Fairish legion have come for us. Finally, we're almost home!"

Duchess looked into the sky and saw the most glorious sight that she had ever seen. Chariots of fire and the colorful flames of celestial dragons lit up the sky and were followed by Fairish soldiers that sparkled in stardust. The celestials and fairies landed in a circle around a gigantic celestial dragon that was attached to a chariot. A high celestial in shining silver armor descended from the chariot and walked hastily over to them. Duchess had never seen anyone so beautiful.

"Proxima, How good it is to see you."

"General Sharaya, you had us all extremely worried to say the least."

"We are glad to be on our way home."

"You both will ride with me. I've personally promised King Zionous that I will see you both to Eucaron safely."

"Thank you, Proxima. We are much obliged. We have gained some companions on our journey. This is Mr. Twill and Chewy."

"Well, I haven't seen a Twill since the days of the Council of Crepusculum. You, the princess, and your small companions shall ride with me."

"Even though we Twills are small creatures, Prince Proxima, we are known for our wit and speed. Why my great grandfather Twill once outsmarted Orion and won his very own constellation to rule."

"I have no doubt, fine Twill. Come let's go quickly.

Murathim is under our protection but we have not set up a perimeter here. Who knows what could be lurking."

"Your Highness, wait."

Proxima Centauri turned to acknowledge his commander.

"We've found these clowns lying in the snow a few feet away."

"Clowns on Murathim? General Sharaya, how is this even possible?"

"They helped us escape from Gateway City and find the gateway to the heavens. They even fought their own fellow soldiers in order to see us to safety."

"Don't trust them!" Duchess yelled out without thinking.

"That one tried to kidnap me!"

Proxima's eyes burned with anger after hearing Duchess' words.

"Commander, lock them up in the cells here on Murathim. I will alert the celestial alliance and King Zionous of their presence. It will be up to them to decide the clowns' fate. Now we must be on our way at once."

General Sharaya, Duchess and their two small companions were quickly escorted to Proxima's chariot and hoisted in. After helping them into the chariot, Proxima took a seat on top of his celestial dragon and they shot into the sky like lightning, leaving the clowns behind them on the frozen planet.

Duchess pulled the warm blankets in the chariot close to her as they flew through space.

"Duchess, are you quite sure that was the clown that tried to nab you in the village? This could mean life or death for them. You must be sure," General Sharaya said.

"That moment is burned into my memory, Sharaya. I'll never forget the moment that changed my life forever."

Back in the Dark Tower

"Help me up yeh worthless rats."

General Madix's soldiers pulled him to his feet and dusted him off.

"Alright, alright. That's enough. I've got to see Epsilon posthaste."

General Madix headed up the stairs and walked right past the door to the gateway. He heard the deylai coming up the stairs behind him and they began to break through the barricade that General Sharaya , Measles, and the others had built. In a few moments, General Madix stood at the door to Epsilon's chamber and knocked loudly.

"Come in, General."

"Epsilon, I 'ave retrieved the star scroll from the fairy. You were right as always. The darn fairy had it on her person."

"Excellent work, General."

General Madix removed the scroll from his pocket and placed it carefully into Epsilon's hand.

Epsilon stared at the scroll with wide eyes and slowly opened it.

"The scroll of High Celestial King Augustus Celenamis. Polus would have given his life before he told me the location of this scroll. I was just a young star when this was written many millennia ago."

Epsilon's Captain of the Guard Cabis entered his chamber.

"Cabis, have they made it to Eucharon with the clowns?"

"Yes, my Lord. The fairy General was able to break through your spell and bring the portal into being. The clowns were with them."

"Good. All has gone according to plan."

8

The Last Song of Aurora Borealis

King Zionous paced in the royal war room where he and General Sharaya sat.

"What are you saying exactly, Sharaya?"

"I'm saying that our escape to Pearl City was far too easy. The trip should have been virtually impossible. I'm starting to think that Epsilon may have something to do with this."

"I must question the clowns immediately. If Epsilon had something to do with your escape, then the clowns are here as his spies."

"Sire, Epsilon has the scroll of Augustus in his possession. I failed to protect it and I've failed to protect our people. I am deeply sorry for my failure."

King Zionous continued to walk back and forth in the war room. He stopped at the window and looked down on Pearl City with a heavy heart.

"When our people left Earth after the old wars and found refuge on Eucaron, I thanked the heavens for a time of peace. Now we are facing annihilation by a force more powerful than we've ever imagined. The star scrolls are the key to ending the reign of the high celestials in all of the realms of all thirteen heavens."

The Clowns Meet Their Fate

"I...I...I dun't think I ever b...b...b...been so c...c...c...cold, Meas. It's not human 'ow they keep us locked up in this icy dungeon. Do yeh think we made a mistake by thinkin' that the fairies would take pity on us?"

"Stay calm now, Pop. I gots an' idea. If only we could talk to the King. It be his own daughter that we saved yeh know."

The clowns heard footsteps coming quickly towards their cell. The creaky dungeon door opened slowly and celestial guards rushed in, grabbed the clowns and pulled them to their feet.

"Unhand us yeh blithering skunk trolls. Where are yeh takin' us? We demand a conference with yer King, posthaste. Posthaste I say!" Measles yelled.

The guards paid no attention to the two squirming clowns

and led them down the cold hallway in silence. At the end of the corridor, the clowns were led up a set of stairs and out into the cold snow. They could see a glass dome in the distance surrounded by soldiers, and tried to prepare for the worst. After what felt like a million years, they finally made it to the dome.

"Do yeh smell that, Pop?"

"Yeah Meas. It smells like fresh bread."

The clowns were led into the center of the dome and were seated at a dressed table with fresh bread, herbed stuffing and sweet potato pie already laid out.

"Unchain them and let them eat."

The clowns were frightened by the voice that seemed to boom from the dark shadows of the dome, but their stomachs got the best of them. The celestial guards quickly unshackled them and the clowns began to eat and drink as they were permitted to. When they saw a small unit of Fairish guards approaching them they quickly stood to their feet.

"Rise for the great King of the fairies, our great Lord of the high and lowlands of earth, water, and sky. King Zionous the triumphant."

Right after the Fairish guardian announced King Zionous, a regal looking fairy with a large crown made of leaves fashioned from white diamond and iron stepped forward and gazed searingly at the two clowns.

"Please do excuse us lowly clowns, King Zionous. We meant no disrespect to yeh, yer highness. We been through quite a debacle. Yeh see, yer highness, I thinks there is some sort of mis...."

King Zionous held up his hand and signaled for Measles to

be silent.

"You will have time to speak your mind, clown. Sit and eat first. As you dine, remember how lucky you are to be alive, after all that you clowns have done to our people. You are seated in the great celestial dome that has seated the celestial councils of past and present. It is here that our great leaders have discussed the fate of the clowns and today I will do the same."

Measles and Popcorn started to feel far less hungry after hearing the King's speech.

"We are thankful for yer kindness, yer majesty. We've always revered the fairies an' Pop an' I were the ones that helped yer daughter an' the General escape to Pearl City."

"Didn't you also try to kidnap my daughter and bring her to Clown Town by force? I must warn you both that this meal is out of my gratitude for saving my daughter and niece, but my kindness will promptly come to an end if you lie to me."

Measles dropped to his knees and grabbed on to King Zionous' robe.

"I was forced, yer great, by the dark wizard Epsilon! I 'ad no other choice, yer highness. You've got to believe me. I mean no one no harm!"

King Zionous peered at the clowns who were now trembling in fear.

"Has Epsilon sent you here as his spies? The cost of your lies will be your lives."

"No, yer highness. We was treated no better than the blasted cattle back in Gateway City. We've come to seek refuge here in the heavens. I know of Epsilon's plan to steal the star scrolls. I can help yeh fight him, I promise. He will plunge the entire universe into darkness!"

King Zionous walked slowly through the echoey empty dome. The fire in the center of the dome crackled loudly during the thick silence. The King stopped and stared out into the icy tundra that surrounded them.

"I am not convinced of your loyalty, clown, but you both will be permitted to stay for now. I assume you also speak for your companion as well?"

"Aye yes, yer majesty. Old Pop 'ere loves the fairies more than any odder clown I know."

"General Ferran and his soldiers will escort you both to Pearl City tonight. I must return at once. Tonight we remember my late wife, Queen Chalay."

The Funeral of Queen Chalay of the Royal Faree

Duchess' eyelids fluttered as she lay in the long blades of plush grass that covered Pearl City. She lazily rolled to her stomach and dipped her finger in the crystal clear waters that flowed through the meadow. She watched as a local clan of turtles marched through the grass and descended into the water. Their hard-shelled bodies moved without a care in the world. Duchess felt a bit of jealousy of the carefree animal. *What a lovely little life. Why wasn't I born a turtle?*

Duchess rubbed her leg and winced in a bit of pain while she stretched her sore muscles. The journey to Eucaron left her feeling utterly exhausted. Now that she had arrived, the news of her mother's death started to weigh on her heavily.

Duchess heard the faint sound of footsteps in the soft grass behind her. King Zionous bent down and touched his daughter's hair.

"Duchess my dear, come. It's time."

King Zionous helped her to her feet and offered Duchess his arm. The two began to walk slowly towards the castle.

"You were too young to remember this meadow, but your mother and I used to spend many a day with you and your sisters here. Listening to the meadow was one of your mother's favorite things to do. Duchess, I want you to know how much I love you and how much I loved your mother. She'll always be with us, and today is a day to celebrate her life. I wish your sisters could be here today for the ceremony but...they'll be with us soon."

King Zionous and Duchess continued to walk in silence until they reached the palace and boarded a carriage pulled by two gigantic shimmering green and blue dragonflies. The carriage immediately shot into the sky surrounded by members of the Fairish military.

"King Zion...I mean father, where are we going?"

"The ceremony will be held at the high celestial palace that is deep within the Capricornus constellation. Look Duchess, we're nearly there."

Duchess stared out of the window of the carriage that flew through space. Shooting stars from every direction were landing in the courtyard of the resplendent palace. The dragonflies glided seamlessly to the ground and the Fairish guardians that accompanied the royal family stood at attention. Felanthiam and Augustus stood at the palace entrance waiting to receive them.

Duchess began to tremble at the sight of the celestials in their grandeur. King Zionous grabbed her hand and led her from the carriage. They stood in front of the carriage and slowly walked towards Felanthiam and Augustus to the sound of drums and horns that surrounded them. King Zionous bowed low before the rulers of their universe and Duchess followed. Felanthiam touched their heads as they bowed.

"My children, we wish you peace during this time of grief and darkness. The universe grieves with you today. Come, let us continue in our tradition and walk to the edge of the galaxy where Aurora Borealis will sing The Last Song."

King Zionous and Duchess slowly rose to their feet and followed Felanthiam and Augustus. Duchess looked behind her and saw thousands of celestials and fairies following them on their journey to the edge of the galaxy. The beat of the drums guided the pace of their steps as the funeral procession lit up the galaxy on their way to the memorial service. King Zionous held his daughter's hand tightly. He leaned in close and whispered to Duchess.

"This journey to the edge of the galaxy is done whenever a fairy or star has fallen. The difficulty of our journey here represents the journey of healing. We use this time to remember the ones that have left us and we say emayao to ourselves as we journey. Emayao means 'soon we'll be home' in the ancient celestial language."

The walk to the edge of the galaxy was long, and the sound of drums echoed through the endless skies of eternal space that lingered above those that marched in the procession. Just as Duchess began to grow weak, she saw an amphitheater at the edge of the galaxy and colorful lights shooting towards the sky from the center. Duchess followed her father and the royal stars to the front row and those that traveled with them began to fill the vast space behind them in a circle. Duchess could not look away from the colorful lights in the center of the amphitheater. Different shades of purple, yellow, pink, green and blue danced in unison until a figure started to emerge from its center. The colorful lights began to transform into cloth that fell to the feet of the figure that was morphing into a woman. Duchess' eyes met with hers, and the woman stretched out her hands to King Zionous and her.

"King Zionous and my dearest Duchess. Our hearts are with you always."

High Celestial King Augustus Celenamis walked to the stage slowly. Those that gathered instantly fell silent at his presence.

"We gather here today to remember the heart, soul, and life of one that loved her family, her kingdom and gave her life in the fight against shadow—Queen Chalay of the royal Faree clan. In this time of fear, we must remember that we are not alone. We will stand against the dark forces of the universe as one, and we will walk into battle with one mind. Aurora Borealis will now sing The Last Song, Emayao."

Aurora Borealis stepped forward and raised her arms towards the sky. The royal Fairish musicians played wind instruments and drums of every kind, and the amphitheater was filled with the most glorious sounds that Duchess had ever heard. Fairish singers walked slowly onto the stage and stood behind Aurora. They hummed a low tune along with the sound of the Fairish instruments. The sounds that came from their lips was an eerie, melodic and melancholy hum that sounded like the voices of ghosts and angels. Aurora Borealis began to sing and Duchess couldn't look away.

> "E-may-a-o, E-may-a-o, E-may-a-o, E-may-a-o
> For one to fall, leaves one to rise.
> May starlight never leave your eyes.
> The way unknown, the journey deep.
> You held my heart and led my feet.
>
> E-may-a-o, E-may-a-o, E-may-a-o, E-may-a-o
> These words are mine, and mine to give.
> Even though my last, with you I live.
> Love never dies, love always lives.
> In our lives, our hearts, our minds, our lips.
>
> E-may-a-o, E-may-a-o, E-may-a-o, E-may-a-o
> The sun will rise, the stars will shine.
> I'll see your face and you'll see mine.
> Forever ends, it's not for long.
> And we'll be there with the stars at home. "

All was silent once the song ended, and the sound of the drums resumed. General Sharaya led the other Fairish Generals onto the stage and they all raised their wands to the sky and lit up the amphitheater with thousands of small capsules of light that shot from their wands. One by one each that attended started to give their condolences to the King and Duchess, then turn and begin their journey back to the celestial castle. Aurora Borealis made her way from the stage, and once she reached Duchess she hugged her tightly. She then spoke to the King, embraced him and joined the procession returning to the palace.

"King Zionous, On behalf of the last celestials of Arokaya, I offer my deepest condolences. My people stand with you as one."

"Thank you, Proxima. It means so much to me that you are here. Duchess, you remember Proxima. May I formally introduce Prince Proxima Centauri Vindematrix from the Arokayan universe. Proxima and I have fought many battles together and he is a close friend and ally."

Duchess did her best to be polite but was overwhelmed by everything that had just taken place. She solemnly held out her hand and gave a slight curtsy.

"My deepest condolences your highness."

"Thank you...Prince Proxima. It is a pleasure to see you again."

With that, Proxima bowed and followed the procession back to the palace. Duchess felt a hand touch her shoulder and turned to see her Uncle Ferran standing behind her in a Fairish General's uniform.

"Uncle Ferran! I can't believe it's you."

Duchess jumped into her uncle's arms and felt the familiar warm scruff of his beard on her face.

"My, my how much you have grown, Duchess. You look just like your mother."

"You've been here all of this time, uncle?"

"Yes, fighting alongside King Zionous here and in the lower heavens. I wish I would have been there to protect you and your mother. We tried everything that we could to bring all of you here for quite some time, but it was just too dangerous to move all of you. Now I don't know what we should have done. Forgive me for not being there, Duchess, to protect you and your mother."

"Oh, Uncle Ferran. I could never blame you. I blame myself for not leaving Clown Town sooner and coming home."

"The clowns would never have let you leave once you were in their grasp, Duchess. You can't blame yourself. Come, I'll accompany you back to the palace."

9

Even the Stars Turn Cold

Duchess squinted her eyes and quickly pulled her blanket over her head to block the bright sunlight that was streaming through her window.

"Sharaya, I'm sure you have better things to do than try to get me out of bed. As you can see I'm perfectly fine. Now please go away!"

General Sharaya sat on Duchess' bed and tried to pull her blankets away.

"Duchess, it's been over a month since the memorial. It's time that you start to learn about Fairish magic and who you are. War is upon us, and we need your help if we are going to beat Epsilon. As we speak, the deylai have pushed back celestial forces from Mars and are ready to attack at any moment."

Duchess uncovered her face angrily.

"Why are you here, Sharaya? I don't have the power to stop Epsilon. He's killed my mother and I've had no word on where my sisters or niece are. They might all be dead as well. I'm just a village girl. How can I help to stop a war?"

"Duchess, listen to me. Every life in the universe wields the power to change the world, but we have to choose to do it. You are here for such a time as this; to face this darkness and help lead our people to freedom and safety from a force that seeks to steal all that is beautiful and sacred from the heavens of light. What choice will you make?"

General Sharaya kissed her cousin on the forehead and rose to leave.

"Remember, Duchess, I am but a simple fairy, but I have led our legions into battle against the forces of the dark. Who am I to say that I am not fit to serve?"

General Sharaya turned and left the room, and Duchess was left alone in her misery yet again. Duchess wanted to cry, but she didn't have the strength to shed another tear. She wasn't sure what to do or where to go in her new home. Everything was different and strange. The noise of her stomach growling reminded her that she had not eaten much lately. Just then, she heard a gentle knock on her door.

"Come in," Duchess said wearily.

A very short, round fairy holding a tray of food wobbled into Duchess' room.

"Sorry to bother you mum, but the General has ordered that we bring you your breakfast."

"Oh yes, well thank you. I am feeling rather famished all of a sudden. It smells wonderful. What is it?"

"Eggs, herbed fried potatoes and fresh biscuits that I baked me self mum. The King requested that you meet him in the courtyard once you've eaten and dressed."

"Of course. Thank you. Would you have a few pieces of bacon that I could also have with my eggs?"

The kitchen maid's face turned slightly pale.

"Uh, no mum. I am sorry, but we fairies do not eat meat. We are strict vegetarians."

"Oh, I am sorry. I...I didn't realize. What you've brought is perfect. Thank you."

The maid curtsied slightly, then scurried quickly from the room. Duchess gobbled up her food, then looked around for her clothes. Fairish clothes were definitely far less extravagant than her Clown Town wardrobe, but were just as beautiful—only in a different way.

She wasn't sure at all what she would be doing with her cousin and father, so she chose a dress made of light fabric that was beautifully embroidered with colorful swans. After washing up and adjusting a blue sash around her waist, she made her way down to the courtyard.

It was a beautiful day, and the air smelled fresher than the air in even the Garden Gate Village. Once Duchess arrived in the yard, a Royal Fairish Guardian went to fetch the King. Duchess sat by the large fountain in the center of the courtyard while she waited for her father. She closed her eyes for a moment and felt the wind whip across her face and flow through her hair.

How much everything has changed, mama. I miss you, she

thought.

"There's my beautiful girl."

King Zionous' powerful voice echoed through the courtyard, and his enthusiasm brought a smile to Duchess' face. Duchess turned and embraced her father warmly.

"You look tired, papa. Is everything alright?"

"The war rages on, but as for today we are lucky to live in safety with our people."

"What about tomorrow? Will we not be safe then?"

"Who knows what tomorrow may hold, my love. All we have is today, so let us give thanks to the ones on high. Today is a grand day, for today you will be given your wand and learn to use your wings. Are you ready, my child?"

Duchess was not at all ready to do any of these things, but the hopeful look in her father's eyes made her feel more at ease.

"Of course I'm ready father."

"Before we begin, I have a gift for you."

The King beckoned for one of his Fairish guardians, and the soldier stepped forward and handed him a long, narrow box.

"Wands are handed down from generation to generation in our clan, and I want you to have your mother's wand. She would want you to have it. It was the most powerful wand in her family."

Duchess held the box in her hand for a moment, then slowly opened it and removed the wand. She held the wand in her hand and rubbed the pearl-laden handle with her thumb.

"I've never held a wand before. It's heavier then I imagined it would be."

The King chuckled.

"Yes, it's made of Eucrachian steel that was fashioned from

star fire. The handle was made from pearls that were collected from the aquarian world of Milandria before it was destroyed. Your mother's star stone and the stones of your ancestors who owned this wand in the past will forever be connected to it, and will always be there to guide you. In time you will learn how to use it. Always remember that your wand is much more powerful when you connect it to your star stone.

Now then, today I want to show you the universe. You must learn about the world you come from if you want to change it. You will also have your first lesson in Fairish magic today, and learn how to call for your wand."

"How will we travel today, papa? I don't see the carriages. Why do I need to call for my wand when I have it right..."

Duchess looked at the box where she had set her wand and it had disappeared.

"Well, I thought it was right here."

"We fairies only use carriages for ceremonial events. In battle or on journeys we fly in formation. Now that I have presented your wand to you it is yours to keep, but wands do not live in the present realm. Today you will learn to use your wings and we will fly to Arokaya, but first you must learn how to call for your wand and summon your wings. Here, I'll show you."

King Zionous stepped forward and raised his arms towards the sky.

"'Felay menaya' is what we say to call for our wands in our clan. It means that we call forth the gift of magic, that the mother of all stars has graciously given to us. The magical words that we speak are not chants as they do in dark magic, but prayers of thanks and recognition that we connect to all things that live and all things that give us life. We ask with a heart of gratitude each and every time that we use our magical words; we never demand. After all, greed is the beginning of black magic. Now, watch me. Felay menaya."

King Zionous spoke the magical words and pulled his wand from thin air.

"You see, Duchess. It's very simple. Now that I have my wand, I must use it to call forth my wings by waving my wand and saying ahalayum, which means 'to be lifted' in Fairish."

The King waved his wand and spoke the Fairish words and his large fairy wings instantly appeared.

"Once our wings have been summoned we say mun haya nanoee as our prayer that our wings will take us safely on our journey and guide us back safely to the ones we love."

Duchess felt overwhelmed by the entire process and wished that she would have grabbed a piece of parchment to write on before leaving her room. The King took note of the worried look on her face and placed his hands on her shoulders.

"Don't worry, my dear. These words and all that I have shown you are part of you. In times of war, legions of soldiers call for their wands and summon their wings together before entering into battle. This ritual and the words that we utter unite us as one. If soldiers can do it before entering into battle, you can surely do it here in the courtyard.

Don't be too hard on yourself. Our people learn our traditions from infancy and you are learning it all now. Why don't you give it a try, alright? I'm right here to help you."

Duchess took a deep breath and held out her arms. She closed her eyes and honed into the sounds all around her.

"Felay menaya," Duchess said.

"Did I do it right?" Duchess squinted as she opened one eye but she didn't see her wand.

"Focus on your star stone, Duchess, and bond it to your wand. Listen to the wind, to the earth, to the stars, and to my voice. What is the universe saying to you?"

Duchess closed both eyes again and thought about her star stone. All she could remember was the pain when Epsilon tried to pull it from her chest. She gasped for air and tried hard not to fall over. King Zionous grabbed onto her and helped her regain her balance.

"I know that all you can think of is the pain when you try to access your star stone, Duchess, but try to let go. Just be still and your magic will come to you," he said.

Duchess squeezed her eyes tightly and focused on the rhythm of the wind. As she stood still for just a moment, she could feel a warm glow in her chest. The warmth started to spread through her arms, move down her legs and then seemed to explode out of her skin and surround her. Everything suddenly grew quiet, like she was in a small room. An image of a clear stone filled with black tar popped into her mind. It was floating in midair and everything else faded away. The black tar in the center of the stone began to drain through the bottom and instantly vanish. Once the stone turned completely clear everything inside her grew calm. Duchess felt the rhythm of the earth and sky pulse through her like she had many life forms living inside of her.

"Do you see your star stone, Duchess? Do you feel it? Epsilon's dark magic is now gone. You can unleash your power and summon your wand now. Don't be afraid, my child. Use the power of those that have gone before you. Your mother will always be with you. Think of her," King Zionous said.

Duchess remembered how safe she felt when she was surrounded by the ones that she loved back in the Garden Gate Village, and she pictured her mother as the reigning Queen of their people. For the first time since her mother had passed, Duchess was grateful for the time they spent together—even though she was no longer alive. Just thinking about this made Duchess feel invincible. She heard a faint whisper that sounded far away. "I love you," it said. Duchess took a deep breath and prepared to summon her wand for the first time.

"Felay menaya."

Duchess instantly pulled her wand from thin air just as her father did.

"I did it, papa!"

"Yes! Now summon your wings, child, and remember to connect your wand to your star stone."

Duchess closed her eyes again and took another deep breath in.

"Ahalayum."

Duchess felt two large wings instantly grow from her back. It was a strange feeling that was neither pleasant or unpleasant. Duchess was surprised how natural she felt with her wings, and wondered how she ever managed without them.

"Don't forget to pray for safety, my dear. Our wings are used to travel and serve the ones we love."

"Oh yes, uh, mun haya nanoee."

"Very good my dear, very good. Remember that faith can

carry you higher and farther than even your wings can. Now let's test them out. Are you ready? Guardians assemble and prepare to take flight!" King Zionous commanded.

A troop of Fairish guardians surrounded the King and Princess as they prepared to fly from Pearl City. The Fairish guardians rose into the sky first and led the way. King Zionous took his daughter's hand and they both lifted off together in formation with the Fairish guardians.

"Hold onto me, my dear. We'll have to fly into the celestial meridian of the great galactic poles and then down into the black gateway of Zenith to reach Arokaya."

Duchess was amazed that she didn't have to try to fly at all. She simply looked to the sky and her wings effortlessly took over. The fairies rose higher and higher until they reached the stars. Duchess was breathless at the sight of all of the stars, moons, and planets that they soared by. A shooting star accompanied them for part of their journey and chatted with King Zionous.

"Good morrow, King Zionous!"

"Plentius, my good friend! It has been too long since I have seen you. You look well!"

"I am well, King Zionous. I am indeed very well. Who is this beautiful child that accompanies you?"

"My daughter Duchess accompanies me today. I am blessed to have her with me in Pearl City, and soon my other daughters will join us."

"Blessed day, King Zionous! Blessed day. Where are you off to this fine day?"

"We journey to Arokaya."

"I do wish you safe travels. I have yet to visit Arokaya since its destruction. Far too depressing of a place these days. I am surprised that you choose to travel there with such light military accompaniment."

"There is no real threat in Arokaya. Proxima has made sure to quell any troll squatters that have tried to take certain parts of the region. My guardians also help to patrol the portals to the other heavens."

"Glad to hear it, King Zionous. I do wish I could accompany you both, but I'm off to the black sands of Oraku for some much-needed relaxation. I bid you farewell and wish you and those you cherish safe travels!"

"Thank you, Plentius. I wish the same to you as well."

With that, the bright star turned and shot off in a different direction.

"This is the most beautiful thing I've ever seen, father," Duchess yelled.

The guardians' wands lit the way while they flew speedily through space and into the black gateway of Zenith.

"Alright Duchess, hold on. We are about to go through the black hole."

Duchess clutched her father's arm tightly and closed her eyes. A strong wind blew harshly against the fairies, but they pressed on through the black hole. When they came out of the other side, Duchess saw pitch black darkness lit by the smoldering blue flames of planets burning in the distance. Not one star was in sight. As they flew further, Duchess saw what looked to be like fields of diamonds; some as big as planets.

"As you can see, even the stars grow cold, Duchess. This is the dead Arokayan universe that was wiped out with Mancai's black flames of the lower heavens. The entire galaxy burned one planet and star at a time. We must go to the dead galaxy of Centaurus to meet Proxima. He and his people have gathered there for a memorial. They are all that is left of the royal celestials of this universe."

Duchess felt sick to her stomach. The air smelled of ash and sulfur, and the toxic smoke from the smoldering planets burned her eyes and throat.

"Father, who is Mancai?"

"Mancai was a powerful star that stood with Celestial King Augustus Celenamis in the days of the council of Crepesculum. He became more powerful than those that were on high and was cast out by King Augustus himself, even though he had a son. Perilous, the Demon Lord of the seventh heaven, took pity on him and made him his heir. He ruled alongside Perilous for many occurrences of the vernal equinox in the first heaven and now seeks for all of the thirteen heavens to be under their rule. Some say he is a demon that communes with the spirit of Ranis, but I remember when he was on high. He was full of light, but became broken and bitter because of the way those on high treated him."

Duchess and King Zionous landed in the ruins of the Arokayan celestial palace where Prince Proxima Centauri had gathered his remaining people. Proxima instantly spotted them and rushed over to where they landed.

"King Zionous, General Sharaya told me that you were coming here and I highly discouraged it, but I am grateful that you have come all this way. Please pardon us, as we are in a time of mourning and deep grief."

"My deepest sympathy to you and your people, Proxima.

We must all never forget the devastation that happened here and work tirelessly to stop Mancai."

"Yes, King Zionous, I do agree."

"I am sorry for your loss, Proxima. To see what one dark star has the power to do is...I have no words to describe it," Duchess said.

"Thank you, Princess, for your kind words. Please forgive me, as I must return to my people."

"Yes, of course. May you one day find peace, my friend. The Arokayans are forever welcome in our universe." Said King Zionous.

Proxima embraced the King and returned to where his people were gathered.

Duchess and the King watched in silence as the celestials sang and wept over the ruins of their home. One of the stars in attendance slipped from the crowd and slowly walked towards them.

"Commander Niran, I didn't realize that you would be in attendance here," said King Zionous.

"Yes, Felanthiam was saddened that she could not come herself, but I've just received word that Felanthiam requires a conference with you at the celestial palace right away. I will accompany you all there now."

"Thank you, Commander. We will go at once."

They all took flight immediately and made their way to the high celestial palace. They touched down in the courtyard and were quickly led by Commander Niran into audience with the high celestial Queen.

"Zionous, thank you for coming. We've just learned that

Epsilon is planning to attack the celestial palace with the help of Mancai."

"How can this be, Felanthiam?"

"Epsilon has mobilized the deylai on Mars, and they will ascend on this palace very soon. We must be ready and prepare the palace's defenses. If he takes the palace, he will soon have this entire universe under his control. We cannot let that happen. I will not let what happened in Arokaya happen here. I will give my life before I see the day that my children's lives are taken from me."

"The fairies will not let that happen, Felanthiam, and we will stand and fight beside our high King and Queen."

"Thank you, Zionous. We will need you now more than ever. I must gather the celestial alliance and meet with Kiranales at once. Epsilon loved her once. Somewhere in his heart that love may still remain."

"We must try all that we can, Felanthiam. I need to gather my Generals. I will accompany you to the council meeting on Murathim."

"Yes, of course. I will send Commander Niran with word of when the meeting will take place. It must be soon. My dearest Duchess joins us in a time of war. Those that are able must all be ready to stand and fight. Go in peace my children."

"Peace to you, mother of all," King Zionous said with a bow.

King Zionous and Duchess exited the presence of the Queen and immediately took flight. Felanthiam walked over to the window and stared into the vast universe in silence. She heard the familiar footsteps of her brother King Augustus and sighed at his presence.

"Look what you've done to us, brother. There would be no Epsilon if it weren't for your foolish pride. To cast out a star that was without blame only because he was stronger than you has brought death to us all."

High King Augustus' eyes burned red with fire, and he turned and stormed from Felanthiam's presence in silence.

* * *

The words of Felanthiam burned in Duchess' chest as they flew back to Eucaron.

Must I really stand and fight? She thought.

No sooner had they touched down in the courtyard of the royal Fairish palace did the chief Fairish guardian run towards them.

"My King, I have news. Our spies have rescued the Princesses and brought them home. They are eating in the great hall as we speak sire."

King Zionous and Duchess ran to the great hall and saw Lez and Thimble Faree eating with Duchess' niece in Lez's arms. Tears rolled down their faces as they ran to embrace them.

10

The Tanatoors Allegiance

"I gotta say, Pop, that this be the life, don't yeh think? I don't even miss meat all that much yeh know it."

"Yes, tis amazin' what the fairies can do with all these 'ere vegetables, innit? The only thin' I miss about 'ome be our clown makeup."

"Aye, Pop. That would be nice, but at least we still 'ave our uniforms, wigs an' noses."

"Do yeh think we'll ever get home again, Meas?"

"Not sure, Pop. Not sure if I even want to, if I was honest an' all. The weather seems real nice 'ere. Watchin' all these 'ere fairies an' animals buzz round is quite a comfort. Relaxin' even."

"Yer right, Meas. The fairies have been real kind to us."

"Aye, Pop. I've grown quite use to these 'ere meadows an' hills an' all. All this fresh air seems to do us well, eh Pop?"

Measles got up, stretched his arms to the sky and yawned lazily. He was turning from side to side stretching his waist when he spotted something in the distance.

"Hey, look over there. Yeh see that, Pop? It looks like a festival of sorts down there in the town. Tell our uh fairy guards to follow us that way."

The clowns and their Fairish guardians wandered into the town and started to poke around the different booths. The clowns found themselves in need of a snack and decided on a booth that had fresh goat milk and pastries.

"Welcome to the town of Brandleberry, gentlemen. May I interest yeh in a fresh glass of goat milk and an apple fritter? It's from me own farm up in the hills of Glassborough."

"I could use me a snack. How 'bout you, Pop?"

"I sure could use a snack me self, Meas. What's yer name kind fella?"

"Me name is Mr. Finnigan of the mountain clan. Me family has cared fer goats an' sheep since we was back on Earth."

"Ah, I see. Is that how this fairy business works eh?"

Mr. Finnigan laughed ferociously as he poured glasses of milk for the clowns and their Fairish guardians. He quickly turned and took out hot apple fritters from the stone oven behind him.

"I'll tell yeh no taradiddle, gents. That I do promise. How do yeh like that milk an' apple fritter?"

"Why it's the best me ever 'ad," Measles said with a mouth full of fritter and milk.

Mr. Finnigan roared with laughter again and slapped his thigh.

"Well to answer yer question laddies, yes, each fairy that yeh see 'ere belongs to a clan. Each clan 'as a duty to care fer a part of the universe. We mountain clans-folk care fer goats an' sheep. Then yeh 'ave the clans of water, forest an' sky. The Faree clan is the royal clan that cares fer the celestials an' protects our people."

"It's quite the beautiful life, Mr. Finnigan," Popcorn said.

"Aye, that it is, lad. Aye, that it is. Where yeh gents be from then?"

"Why we're clowns, sir. Excuse our appearance. We seem to have yet to acquire proper clown makeup 'ere."

"I've 'eard stories of the clowns, but can't say I ever laid eyes on one of ya's. You gents don't seem too bad. Not bad at all."

"Our humble thanks, sir. Our humblest of thanks," Measles said with a bow.

"It looks like yer friend 'ere needs a word with yeh."

Mr. Finnigan nodded his head towards the stern Fairish guardian that was quickly approaching the clowns.

"Clowns, we must head back to the palace immediately."

"Alright, alright now we're goin'. What do we owe yeh Mr. Finnigan, fer yeh kind hospitality?" Measles said wiping his mouth.

"It's on me laddies, since yeh be guests of our great King. May yeh be well, gents. May yeh be well."

The clowns guzzled down their remaining goat milk and apple fritters, then were escorted back to the palace by their Fairish guardians just as the sun began to set. The clowns gazed at the sky in amazement on their walk back to the palace.

"Do yeh see the colors of the sunset? I ain't never saw somethin' so beautiful in me life. At least we're not locked in a prison. Just under house arrest is all. We can still look at sights as lovely as these, don't yeh think, Pop?"

"Yes indeed, Meas. Could be far worse."

The clowns were returned promptly to their room once they returned to the palace. They tried asking the guards what was going on, but the Fairish guardians remained silent. The clowns mulled around their room and read a few scrolls that were given to them on Fairish history and magical natural elements. The sun had fully set, and the clowns lazily lounged by the fire and snacked on bits of dried fruit.

"That goat milk seems to 'ave plum tuckered me out, Pop. I thinks I will get me some shut eye. Good night, sleep tight, Pop."

* * *

"I see your mind. I am in your thoughts. You cannot escape me."

"Who's there? Where am I?"

"You think that you can betray me, clown? I have more power than you can fathom. I hold your destiny in my strong right hand, and I will bring your world to extinction."

Measles tried hard to open his eyes, but they were sealed tightly. All that he could see was darkness.

"Epsilon? Please, please, I beg you. I never meant to turn

against yeh. The fairies 'ave captured us."

"Do not lie to me you fool! I see your mind!"

Measles felt a sharp pain pierce his head and cried out, but he could not move or open his eyes.

"There is nowhere you can hide where I cannot find you and make you surrender your will to me. You are mine and forever will be."

Measles cried out again, but was still unable to move.

"Help me! Pop, are yeh there? Help! Help! Someone help me please!"

"Stop crying out, you coward. No one can hear you. I am in your mind—your dreams—and no one has the power to stop me."

"Please Epsilon, spare me life an' I will serve yeh for all me days. I'll do whatever yeh want me to do just please let me be."

"Listen closely to me, clown. You will journey to Haknami in the seventh heaven and retrieve the scroll of ash and shadow from the Demon Lord Perilous and deliver it to me. Do you understand?"

The pain that Measles felt started to melt away, but he was trembling in fear.

"Yes...yes I understand yeh, me Lord. I'll get yeh the scroll. I promise yeh I'll do it."

Measles' eyes fluttered open and he jumped out of his cot. He tried hard to catch his breath, but he still couldn't breathe. He ran for the door and pounded on it.

"Guards! Guards! I need to speak with the King. Guards!"

Measles pounded on the room door where they were held until a Fairish guardian opened it.

"What is it, clown? The King is not able to see you. He has

left for Murathim to speak to the celestial alliance."

"I just got to speak to him...all of 'em there now! Please yeh gotta 'elp me. Epsilon came to me in a dream. I can still 'ear him I tell yeh. I gotta warn 'em!"

"I will get word to General Sharaya. Now stand back, clown."

The creaky room door shut again, and Measles stumbled back into his cot.

"Oh Measles. Did the wizard hurt yeh friend? It'll be alright, I just know it," said Popcorn.

"We'll never be free of him, Pop. We must go to the seventh heaven an' retrieve a scroll. I don't see no way out of it."

"You must be mad, Meas. The fairies won't just let us go on a mission fer Epsilon."

"We gotta convince 'em that we're doin it fer them. Don't yeh see, Pop. It's the only way to survive."

It seemed like forever until the door to the clowns' room opened and General Sharaya entered.

"Get dressed," she said. I have orders to take you both to Murathim. You must tell me exactly what happened on our way there. Get dressed quickly. We haven't much time."

* * *

Felanthiam walked into the center of the room and sent a ball of fire into the magnificent chandelier that lit the entire glass dome on Murathim.

"I call this meeting of the celestial alliance to order. It is in a time of darkness and uncertainty that we gather here today. Great evil has consumed our world, and we must stand and fight.

Epsilon and his army will ascend upon the celestial castle very soon and we must be ready. We need reinforcements. I propose that we recruit additional forces in this heaven and the other heavens of light."

Arev laughed haughtily.

"You are hysterical, mother. Who can stand against the celestials that are on high?"

"Here, here," the council members shouted.

"Arev, do not be blinded by your own arrogance. Those who sit on high can be made low. Who here has not seen the ruins of Arokaya; a universe made destitute by Mancai," said Felanthiam.

"If I may, your highness, I would like to address the council."

"Of course, Orion. Please speak. You have the floor."

"There is a prophecy written in the stars of the lowest heaven of the second coming of a dark force that will rise out of the Lyanthryan pit. This being will unite the dark forces as one, and bear the power to open the thirteenth scroll. It can only be one that the prophecy speaks of, since it was her blood that sealed the scroll."

"You have misread the stars, brother," Arev scoffed.

"Members of the divine celestial alliance, I will lead the most powerful suns of the thirteen heavens into battle against Epsilon, and we will squash his power once and for all!" said Arev.

"Here, here," the council members shouted and rose to their feet in applause.

Felanthiam began to yell above the cheers of the council.

"Silence! Be still, you arrogant fools, and heed to wisdom! Epsilon's forces are stronger than even the most powerful suns in the thirteen heavens. We must unite as one in order to conquer him."

King Augustus raised his staff and the room went silent.

"The Twill desires a word with the council," Augustus' voice boomed and echoed across the dome. The council members took their seats and all eyes turned to Mr. Twill.

Mr. Twill clasped his short stubby hands behind his back and solemnly walked into the center of the dome.

"Thank you, your majesties. Even though we do not see a wave or ripple, 'fish swim below still waters,' as the Twills say. Such are the times that we live in now. Evil lurks beneath us and we must recognize its existence in the thirteen heavens. Normandeery is no longer a safe place for the Twills. The celestial castle will soon come under siege. This war is bigger than all of us here in this room. Pride comes before the fall, but those who stand together can rise as one."

Mr. Twill walked silently back to his seat, and the gentle clopping of his feet rang through the room that had fallen silent.

"Thank you for that fine speech, Mr. Twill. Your wisdom is much needed in this dark time. I've heard from General Sharaya that one of the clowns that has come to us has been contacted by Epsilon. Commander Niran, bring them forward if you please," Felanthiam commanded.

Commander Niran and Fairish guardians brought Measles and Popcorn into the center of the room.

"Must we listen to these clowns blabber on, mother? What is the point of all of this?"

"Quiet, Arev," Felanthiam hissed. "Please speak clowns."

"Well, uh, yer majesties, I been contacted by the wizard through a dream an' I've located the scroll of ash an' shadow. With the court's permission, I'd like to retrieve it."

Felanthiam rose to her feet.

"What is this you are telling us, clown? You wish to journey to where the Demon Lord rules to capture a scroll for the high celestials? What has spurred such grand courageous loyalty?"

"Well yer, uh, yer great one, Epsilon has betrayed us, so we will betray 'im. We would 'ave been Martian food if it wasn't fer the General and Princess. We owe yeh our lives, I guess."

Felanthiam laughed loudly.

"Well then, I say we give them a starship and let them leave right away. All in favor say 'aye'."

The celestial alliance replied, "aye," in agreement.

"It has been decided. Commander Niran, take the clowns down to the starships and get them ready for their mission. We expect to hear a full report on your return, and we wish you success." Felanthiam said.

The clowns were immediately whisked away by celestial guards before they could utter another word.

"Mother, why have we just allowed these clowns to journey to the lower heavens? I thought you commanded all of us to heed to wisdom?" Arev said in a sneering tone.

"Be still, Arev. I suspect that Mancai and Epsilon's alliance is soon coming to an end if he is making this request. Haknami is an ally of Mancai's dark kingdom, yet Epsilon has not gone himself to fetch the scroll."

"Ah, I see. So you have sent the clowns to meet their doom?"

"The clowns have their place in this war. It's up to them what that place will be. I have sent them to carry out a mission that they insisted upon. It is more important now than ever that I speak to the Tanatoors. Princess Kiranales has agreed to accompany me to their realm and speak to them on our behalf. Brothers and sisters those in favor of the recruitment of the Tanatoors say 'aye'."

The celestial alliance replied, "aye," in agreement.

"Thank you, my brother and sisters. We will not let you down. We will be able to defend the celestial palace if the Tanatoors are on our side. As for Normandeery, we must relocate the Twills as soon as possible."

"Felanthiam, the Twills are welcome to find refuge on Eucaron. We will see to it that they arrive safely."

"Thank you, King Zionous. The meeting of the celestial alliance shall now come to a close," Felanthiam said.

"Pardon me mother, but we have not yet voted on the battle of the suns."

"Arev, this is not wise. Mancai has returned and his power alone is stronger than the power of even the thirteen suns."

"Nothing is stronger than the power of the sun! I challenge the alliance to vote now," said Arev.

"All in favor say, 'aye.' Again, all in favor say, 'aye,' or do forever hold your peace. Let the silence of the council show that your request has been denied. We will wait to defend the heavens until Epsilon advances on the celestial palace. Stand by for war plans. This meeting will now conclude," said Felanthiam.

Arev jumped from his seat and rushed from the council room in anger.

"The greatest thirteen suns in the thirteen heavens and I will meet Epsilon in battle. It will be the battle of the suns and we will end this war."

11

The Dark Forces of the 7th Heaven

"Good job, Meas!" said Popcorn.

Measles laughed aloud as he piloted the starship through space.

"This ship flies itself pretty much, yeh know it. Only a wee bit of managin' tis required. This parchment that the guards gave us will lead us to wherever 'as been written on it. I thinks that's what they said, anyways. Read what the celestials wrote won't yeh, Pop. Whereabouts will we be headin' from 'ere?"

Popcorn grabbed the piece of parchment that the celestial guards had given them and nervously opened it.

"Well let me see 'ere, uh. We are on our ways to the uh...

uh black...looks to be the black gateway of Ze-n-ith. From there, we pass through Aro-ka-ya-ya and make our way to the, uh...I can't quite make this word out. Sril-i-ni-ya star fields, an' there we will enter a portal that will take us to the seventh heaven."

"I guess we should sit back an' enjoy the ride then, Pop. Let's see what food rations they packed fer us, eh."

Measles opened a small compartment in the back of the starship and surveyed its contents.

"Well, it looks like we got some raisins, seeds an' tea biscuits."

"You don't see nothin' else? How we sposed to live on just that now?" said Popcorn.

Measles snatched a pack of tea biscuits and squeezed himself back into the small pilot's seat in the small ship.

"I guess we'll just 'ave to make do. Here, I'll split this with yeh."

Measles tossed Popcorn half of his tea biscuits, and the two clowns sat huddled in the cold starship that whirled through space. The clowns jumped up to look out the window when they felt the ship start to shake.

"Here we go now, Pop. We made it to the black 'ole. Hold on tight now."

The clowns jumped back into their seats and buckled their seat belts. The starship shook as it made its way through the black hole. Thankfully it only took a few seconds until it made it to the other side.

"Have yeh ever seen anythin' like this in yer life, Pop? Where are we?"

Popcorn scrambled again to find the parchment that charted

their course.

"It looks like we be in the Aro-kay-an galaxy, but nothin' is 'ere. All these planets and stars look burnt out. There's nothin' 'ere, Meas."

The clowns were busy peering out of the window of the starship at the ruins of the dead stars and planets that whizzed by them, when their ship came to a screeching halt.

"What in all tarnation be 'appenin!" Measles shouted.

"I...I dunno, Meas. I don't see nothin' around fer us to hit."

The ship began to slowly float into the direction of a nearby smoldering planet. Measles looked out of the window and saw life forms gathered on the burnt planet. One of them was guiding the ship in with what seemed to be some sort of magical force.

"Who are they, Meas? I never seen nothin like 'em before."

"Not sure, Pop. They look like monsters out of one of the stories that me mum used to read to me."

The starship clunked down onto the ground and was quickly surrounded. A large pair of claws ripped into the ship and tore off the door like it was paper. All the clowns could see were an endless sea of red and yellow eyes as they were dragged out of the ship and dropped at the feet of a giant creature.

"Arokaya is now under my rule. You are trespassers, and for that you will be punished."

Measles tried hard not to shake at the sound of the frightening voice above him.

"We was on our way to the seventh heaven, great one. We didn't mean to disturb anythin' at all."

"Arokaya is no longer a dead universe and is now under the rule of I, Perilous, the Lord of all Demons. My brethren and I have risen up from the seventh heaven to claim this universe. I was told that the clowns were coming to seek an audience with me."

The Demon Lord towered over the clowns and stared at them with ominous red eyes. He crouched down and looked closely at the clowns. Measles tried hard not to stare at his large horns that were decorated with teeth and bones.

"I've never seen a clown. Funny looking creatures you are. Why do you journey all of this way to see me? Speak!"

"We bring a message from Epsilon. He be requestin' the scroll of ash and shadow."

Perilous scratched his cracked red chin and rose to his feet.

"There is a prophecy that is written in the stars of the twelfth heaven that says the lower heavens will rise to overtake the almighty. Those on high will be brought to the ground and bow low before those that they have cast upon death.

I still remember when Epsilon crashed onto Haknami many years ago. He was young and weak, but his heart was on fire and his fury gave him strength. Although he is strong, he will never be stronger than Mancai. He lacks the deep darkness and black will that the Lords of the dark see in Mancai. It was Mancai, his father, that blotted out the light in this universe with his strong right hand. Epsilon lacks the will to wield the power of the star scrolls. The scroll of ash and shadow will be given to Mancai for he has proven himself worthy.

As for both of you, we must find use for you since you have journeyed all this way. Commander Meggido, see that your men take these two to the Srilinaya Star Fields, and put them to work in the troll pits."

"Please, yer great. We are servants of Epsilon. We come in peace."

The demons dragged the clowns to a transporter which took off for the Srilinaya Star Fields immediately.

* * *

"Get in there, yeh slime."

The clowns were thrown roughly into a dark dungeon. Measles and Popcorn tried to get to their feet. They heard faint yelps as they tried to find their footing on the floor. Their eyes slowly began to adjust to the light of one dim torch that burned in the corner, and the faint forms of other prisoners in filthy rags lying on the cell floor were revealed. They had been stepping on them as they tried to get to their feet. Measles was finally able to use the bars on the door to pull himself to his feet, and he banged on the door of their cell.

"Let us out! We done nothin' wrong! We are servants of Epsilon! We ain't done nothin wrong I tell yeh!" he screamed.

Measles slumped down in a corner of their crowded cell and buried his head in his hands.

"What'll we do now, Pop? I don't even know where we are, or what these demons are gonna do to us."

Measles and Popcorn jumped at the sound of a loud hacking cough coming from the opposite corner of the dark dungeon.

"The pits. They send hordes of us to work in the troll pits to harvest. Have yeh never 'eard of the Srilinayan wars?" the raspy voice said.

The clowns stared blankly at the old, decrepit stranger.

"Well, I'm guessin' yeh haven't. Long ago in the ancient

116

wars, the celestials of the Arokayan universe fought Mancai an' his forces. At the beginning of the war, the Trolls of Alniyah rose through the portal in the Srilinaya Star Fields an' battled the celestials. The trolls bodies 'ave been preserved all of these years by a gas that the stars released when they was destroyed. Troll parts are harvested fer the demons of Haknami."

"What type of...parts are yeh speaking of friend?" asked Popcorn.

"All kinds a parts! Legs, arms, toenails, tongue...Those blasted devils love themselves a juicy troll tongue to fillet!" the old stranger shouted.

"Are yeh tellin' us, sir, that we be harvestin' toenails an' tongues from trolls that 'ave been dead fer a million years?"

The old man coughed again uncontrollably and reached for a tin cup of dirty green water.

"Exactly, me boy. Try to get some shut-eye now. They'll be comin' to bring us to the pits in just a few hours."

Measles and Popcorn sat quietly in their cell and didn't sleep a wink. As the old man said, the demon guards came for them and marched everyone out of the cell and up into the transport that would take them to the troll fields. The ride to the troll fields was short but bumpy. As soon as the transport hit the ground, the prisoners were dragged out and each were given a sack and a sharpened rock.

"Get to work, all of you! Every prisoner must fill their sack, or else no troll broth for any of you," a demon guard yelled.

"Psst...psst. Both of yeh, follow me. I'll show yeh where all of the juicy ones are."

The old man that Measles and Popcorn befriended in their

cell waved them over to where he was standing.

"Thank yeh, friend. What's yer name?" Measles inquired.

"I remember I was as lost as a puppy dog when I first arrived 'ere. Me name is Captain Naman."

"Nice to meet yeh, Captain. I'm Measles an' this is Popcorn. How did yeh find yerself 'ere?"

Captain Naman walked boldly over to a troll body and began to remove its thick toenails and put them in his bag with eerie precision.

"Well, me was a pirate cap'n of a ship that sailed in the land of the Tanatoors. Our ship was caught in a typhoon, and we was sucked into a gateway to this heaven. We was brought 'ere after we was captured. I was separated from me crew when we tried to break out of the dungeon. All be cursed if yeh kill me in this blitherin' rat hole yeh scoundrels!" Captain Naman shouted in the direction of the demon soldiers that were well out of earshot.

"Alrighty then. This one 'as been harvested," Captain Naman said with a final tug of a big toenail.

"If yeh see any o' them blue space maggots crawlin' around grab a few. They be good fer roastin an' go well with the troll broth that we'll be gettin' later fer dinner. This really be paradise fer the demons of haknami. Trolls as far as the eyes can see fer harvestin an' eatin. Now hurry up, yeh two. We gotta each fill our sacks to get troll broth."

The clowns and their new friend scrambled to fill their sacks before the end of the day when they were marched back to their prison cells.

"Cheer up, lads. The demons let us roast our maggots in their great fire pit after a day's work if we fill our sacks. They do 'ave a knack fer tellin' stories, I must say. Sometimes we sits around the fire listenin' to 'em," said Captain Naman.

The tired clowns and Captain Naman stood in line for troll broth, then plopped by the fire to roast their maggots.

"Well bless the stars these aren't too bad, I tell yeh. Tastes just like chicken. It's nice to have a bit of meat again. Even though they be maggots an' all," said Measles.

"Pipe down, yeh two blowhards. The demon Commander is about to speak," said Captain Naman.

The demon army beat on their shields as the large demon Commander made his way to the center of the gathering. He stood proudly looking upon his troops, then raised his hands to silence them.

"Soldiers, Iona Draconis has granted us a new home in Arokaya that will sustain us until the right ascension of the stars of the Arokayan celestial meridian! Let us give thanks."

The demons cheered loudly and the Commander raised his hands again to silence them.

"'Fiaca vexme-drago' was spoken by the ancient dark forces that were sent forth by Iona Draconis. It is the vow that we take to never forget where we come from. Our stories of times of old help us to remember and to crush those that oppose us.

Today I will tell the story of how darkness was born into the thirteen realms.

In the beginning there was darkness, and there is no light without it. Before even the demons came to be, there were two faceless forces that wandered to and fro in a single heaven. These forces grew in power and tried to overtake each other until they one day fled to the opposite sides of their infinite space and raced to build another heaven, then another, then another, until the thirteen heavens as we know them were created. The two forces finally met again in the thirteenth heaven and fought for one million sidereal years for the power to control the thirteenth heaven. Each time they clashed, sparks flew from the force of both of their powers combined. They crashed into each other until they exploded, and their shattered remnants scattered across the other twelve heavens. One spark escaped and flew into the black hole of Zenith. The speed and pressure of the black hole set fire to the passing fragments and the first star was born. The first star was the light that pushed back the dark force Iona Draconis to the lower heavens, but our great deity holds the six lower heavens to this day. The thirteenth heaven will one day no longer be the great abyss! We will take control of the last free heaven and unite all heavens under the mighty power of Iona Draconis!"

The demons stood to their feet and roared with delight, then began to dance around the fire to the beat of the drums in the distance. Popcorn leaned over and whispered to Measles.

"I think we should be headin' back to our cells now, don't yeh think Meas?"

"I agree, Pop. Let's go."

Just as the clowns rose to leave, they heard a ferocious roar come from the sky that sounded like the roar of a thousand soldiers. They looked to the sky and saw dragons made of star fire coming towards them. The demons began to grab their weapons and fire arrows into the sky, but nothing phased the creatures of celestial fire. The dragons breathed fire on the demons and they began to scatter. Measles and Popcorn stood frozen with fear until Captain Naman woke them from their stupor.

"What yeh standin' around gapin' fer? Run, run you fools, like yer life depends on it!"

The three ran towards the dungeon to hide, but a gigantic dragon touched down right in front of them. He sat on his haunches calmly and watched as Measles, Popcorn, and Captain Naman ran frantically into the transport that brought them to the troll fields, hoping that the dragon wouldn't see them. They dove under the seats of the transport and awaited their doom. Suddenly, they felt the transport being lifted from the ground and heard the beat of dragon's wings.

"What's happenin'?" Popcorn cried.

"The dragon be carriyin' us off, that's what! Carryin' us off to be his next meal!" Measles answered.

"Why would he want to eat little old us? We can't be fer much nourishment. Don't yeh think, Meas?"

"I agree with yeh, Pop but that's all that I can imagine he would want us fer."

Captain Naman chimed in.

"If he wanted to eat us, boys, he woulda gobbled us up already! Look down below. My golly I know this place. The dragon be takin' us to the land of the celestial dragons in the world between earth and sky."

12

Ammon and the World Between Earth and Sky

Measles and Popcorn trembled in fear as they felt the dragon slowly touch the ground. They could hear the sound of the mighty dragon's breath, and see the smoke from the small flames of fire that came from his mouth when he exhaled. The clowns and Captain Naman watched the large beast walk over to a crystal clear waterfall that flowed into a great pool, and drink deeply of the fresh water. The dragon turned slowly, sat on his haunches and faced them.

"Stop cowering and come stand before me. I will not hurt you."

The clowns were not quite sure what to do. They ducked down into the transport and hoped that the dragon would somehow go away.

"Come on, yeh lily-livered cowards. We must face this beast."

Captain Naman stood tall, walked out of the transport and stood right in front of the great dragon.

"Do you speak for your companions, human?" the great dragon inquired.

"I speak fer no one but me own self. I am Captain Naman, sir. Pirate Lord of the Tanatoorian seas. I am but yer humble servant, me Lord."

The dragon peered at the pirate Lord without saying a word. He raised his head high and straightened his broad, scaly shoulders. Five other dragons flew from the sky and landed near him. Two of them carried a large golden crown and set it before the great dragon's feet, bowing low to the ground.

"I am Ammon, King of the celestial dragons and ruler of the land and seas in this world between earth and sky."

The great dragon placed the crown that lay before him on his head in a regal manner. Captain Naman laughed loudly and slapped his thigh.

"Why we's all thought Ammon was a sea snake. That's how the folk tale goes, yeh know it."

Captain Naman removed his hat and burst into song.

"In the midst of fog, sod an' stone. Dwells a sea snake named Ammon. Ammon lives in the sea that lies between the world of earth an' sky. It is a place where one has to fly.

To get to that place every man must know. You must go to

the place that reflects where the stars call home."

"A sea snake?" Ammon raised his scaly eyebrow and scratched his beard.

"Some have confused our kind with the Tanatoors. I dare say that the legend may have been born the time that I took a swim in the Sea of Flowers many, many years ago. Enough of this buffoonery. Call your companions to come and stand before me."

Captain Naman whistled and beckoned the clowns to join him. Measles and Popcorn reluctantly left the transport and joined Captain Naman who was smiling ear to ear.

"Who are you? Speak."

"We are clowns yer eh...yer high...one. Me name is Measles Bloghorn, an' this be Popcorn Cobbin. We be from the famous Clown Town."

"And what brought you across space and time to be captured by the demons of Haknami?"

Measles scratched his head and kicked a stone on the rocky ground.

"Well, uh, it kinda be a long story. It 'as been quite a journey fer us."

"The thirteen heavens are no longer one, and even the heavens of light have become divided. Whom do you all serve?" Said King Ammon.

"Well as fer me, King, we Tanatoorian pirates are loyal to the celestial alliance now an' fer-ever more!"

Captain Naman ended his grand speech with a bow. King Ammon nodded his head in approval and turned his gaze back to the clowns.

"I'll handle this, Pop," Measles whispered.

"Yer greatness, we clowns come from a great heritage. Our great King Clownington of old led us to victory in the ancient war against the fairies. Our people are a proud people, but I feel like we 'ave lost our way. Our alliance with Epsilon will bring death to us and everythin' that me father an' grandfather fought fer. I sees that now, an' we pledge our allegiance to the high celestial alliance."

King Ammon peered at the clowns. Small puffs of smoke came from his nostrils as he breathed deeply.

"All of you take a knee. General Crone, bring me my sword."

Another dragon stepped forward with a sword the size of a castle beam in its mouth. King Ammon grasped it firmly in his right claw.

"This sword of my father, and his father before him was forged in the star fire of Felanthiam Celenamis. It is strong and true as you all must be from this day forward."

King Ammon raised his sword over the heads of the clowns and Captain Naman.

"I call all of you to leave who you once were and become who you are meant to be. I hereby declare you Captain Naman and you Measles and you Popcorn, knights of the celestial dragons. You are now tasked with upholding truth and justice in the universe, and defending the high heavens alongside my army of the celestial dragons. What say you?"

All three in unison cried, "Aye!"

"Now rise, war is upon us. Felanthiam calls us to defend the celestial castle. Captain Naman, you must gather your fighters and meet us in the fourth quadrant. We must all don our armor and fly to Felanthiam's aid. My dragons and I will accompany her to meet with Arev.

* * *

Jax Clownington sat miserably in the bumpy carriage while the large horses trotted along the narrow path to Witch Kingdom. He tried to close his eyes, but was jolted awake by yet another bump in the road.

"I still don't know why we are forced to travel to the kingdom of witches so primitively. It's none of Epsilon's business how we retrieve the scroll."

General Madix tried his best not to glare at the now King of Clown Town and chose to stare out the window instead.

"It twas needed, yer excellency. If the fairies or high celestials were to 'ear of our traveling to the kingdom of witches fer the star scroll, we'd be 'avin a battle on our hands. We should be arrivin' soon."

The two clowns sat in silence yet again, both bitterly entangled with their own thoughts.

"How is yer dear sister, yer majesty? I 'aven't seen nor 'eard anythin' from her since the uh...tragic accident."

Jax laid his head back, closed his eyes and placed his clown nose on the seat beside him.

"She is...adjusting to the new circumstances. She will re-emerge in time. Janice will be Queen Regent of the villages that have come under our rule, and I expect her to perform her duties and make sure that the villages are under control."

"Indeed my King, indeed. Will she be attendin' the Royal Winter Promenade then?"

"You do vex me, General Madix, with your questions. Do not forget that I am now your King. Janice will do what she is told to do."

"Of course, yer highness. I meant no disrespect to yer authority an' presence. My deepest regrets, yer majesty," said General Madix dryly.

"Now, tell me about who we'll be meeting with upon our arrival," said Jax

General Madix pulled a piece of paper from his pocket and attached a pair of spectacles to his nose.

"Well, let's see now. It looks like Mercuriel is the leader of the most powerful house in the kingdom, which is the House of Grimorie. He serves as the regent of Witch Kingdom an' is able to commune with Vangemtra. We will meet with him an' the keeper of the scrolls.

Dungeon Master Druix will also give us an update on Truffles' uh...keeping. Is always a lively event to see the witches, sire. They usually cook up some sort of entertainment."

"Yes...lively indeed. I suspect that they have not yet heard the news of my father's death. I will have to break the news to them and convince Mercuriel that establishing an alliance with the clowns is in their best interest," said Jax.

"I mean no disrespect, yer majesty, but what will yeh tell them if they ask yeh how he croaked?" said General Madix.

"My father used to say that silence can bring the strongest man to his knees. I will know how to answer when I meet this Mercuriel fellow. He may respect that I took the crown from my father by force and ended his reign. I will make him realize that I will be a greater King than even my father and grandfathers.

Madix, shut the window on your side will you? There is a coldness in this region unlike any I've ever felt before," said Jax.

The clowns rode in silence for the remainder of the trip. Jax's eyes flew open at the sudden sound of the horses hoofs on the cobblestone ground of the courtyard in front of the enchanted castle of Witch Kingdom. Jax pulled his large fur coat around him and solemnly followed General Madix from the carriage. Two men in long purple robes stood at the doorway to the castle.

"Welcome, King Clownington. Mercuriel awaits you in the throne room."

The clowns followed the two men into the throne room. The large doors creaked as they opened, and the clowns walked down the long aisle to the great black throne made of onyx.

"Great King, we welcome you to the land of the witches and we mourn the death of your father along with you and your people."

Mercuriel bowed before Jax with a fixed gaze from his white eyes.

"I see the news of my father's untimely death has spread far and wide. Many thanks for your condolences," said Jax.

Mercuriel laughed.

"Yes, untimely indeed. I hope that you had a pleasant journey. We will soon dine in the great hall. We have much to discuss."

"Yes Mercuriel, we do. I am curious to know more about you and the houses that make up this great kingdom. My father never spoke of the witches, but your kingdom looks to be thriving. This castle is glorious. I've never seen such a grand throne, and what an interesting stone tablet above it."

Mercuriel stepped over to the black throne and gazed upon the stone tablet.

"This stone was fashioned in the black flames of Lyanthra and was brought to earth by our father Mancai. Its inscription was made by the dead souls of Lyanthra that have foretold the second coming of our great Queen, Vangemtra."

"From what I recall, Vangemtra was a witch from the fairy tales I used to hear as a child. You make it sound like she is real," said Jax chuckling slightly.

"She is very real, King Clownington. Since she sacrificed her life to seal the thirteenth scroll her legacy has become nothing more than a child's nightmare. I have the honor of being possessed by her spirit, and have been given the power to commune with her. As the souls of Lyanthra have foretold, the power of the thirteen suns will resurrect her very soon. Come, let us make our way to the great hall. I have a great feast prepared for you and your travel party, and a very special treat for you all."

Jax and his travel party followed Mercuriel and the robed knights of the house of Grimorie into the great hall and took their seats. Mercuriel clapped his hands and servants began to lay food on the table. Jax did his best to look pleasant, but the smell of the food made him feel nauseated.

"My friends, please enjoy the delicacies of our great kingdom. We have endless platters of eye of newt and fingerling troll soup with wart sauce."

Jax stared at the floating eyeballs in his thick green soup and wondered how he was going to eat the food set before him.

"King Clownington, is everything ok with your plate? I

know that our traditional food is very different from what you are accustomed to in Clown Town. I can have the chefs fix you a different plate if you'd like?"

"Nonsense, Mercurial. This looks excellent."

Jax picked up his spoon and began to gulp down his soup with a smile.

"Excellent. I do have quite the treat planned for tonight."

Mercuriel beckoned for his captain of the guard and ordered him to summon Druix, the Dungeon Master.

Druix appeared in the great hall and walked towards Mercuriel. His long ragged robes dragged slowly behind him.

"Master Druix please sit with us. I'd like to introduce you to King Clownington VII."

Druix slowly turned his gaze towards Jax and reached his hand towards him. Jax wasn't sure if he was dead or alive. He looked like a walking corpse with dead white eyes and long dreaded gray hair.

"It's very nice to meet you, Master Druix," said Jax with as cheery a tone he could possibly muster.

"Master Druix is a legendary Dungeon Master, and has done wonders with our clown prisoner. In fact, we liked him so much that he has become our official court jester. Master Druix, please start the show!" said Mercuriel.

Druix walked slowly to the center of the great hall and raised his hands. The old man began to whisper incantations that were echoed by other invisible voices in the room. The doors of the great hall creaked as they slowly opened, and a very haggard looking Truffles walked into the great hall dressed in a tattered jester costume. Druix motioned for Truffles to stop and Truffles stopped in the center of the room.

"What do you have planned for our special guests today, clown?" said Druix.

Truffles eyes were blank and his bobbed up in response to Druix's question.

"I will do what you will me to do, master," Truffles said in an anguished tone.

"Good, very good. Why don't you show us your box of toys, clown," said Druix.

Truffles stumbled over to a trunk that was brought in and took out a tricycle and three balls. He began to ride the tricycle around the great hall while juggling the three balls. Mercuriel and the members of his house that were present roared with laughter at the sight. Truffles rode the tricycle, juggled, danced and sang until the witches had their fill of laughter. Druix lowered his hands and Truffles instantly dropped to the floor. Jax jumped from his seat and ran over to him.

"Truff, Truff. Can you hear me?"

Truffles looked weak and frail. His eyes were closed and he began to cough.

"Jax," he muttered weakly, "is that you? Help me...please."

Jax stared at his fellow clown helplessly until General Madix pulled him away.

"My deepest apologies, Mercuriel, but it seems the King 'as taken ill. I must get him to his chambers."

"Of course, General. My Captain of the Guard will show you the way. We will meet tomorrow with the keeper of the scrolls. I know that Epsilon expects the scroll of the kingdom of witches as soon as possible."

General Madix pulled Jax along out of the great hall, followed by the rest of their travel party.

"Calm yerself, King Clownington. If we want to win this war we need Mercuriel and his house as our allies. You cannot afford to show weakness to a clown that 'as betrayed yer own people." said General Madix.

Jax pulled away from General Madix.

"Get your hands off of me! It's despicable. A clown with royal blood should never be paraded in front of strangers in that manner. It's an insult to us all. Our forefathers have been bound to the dark stars and witches because of their great power for centuries, and it's time that we rise above these primitive beings. We will find our own source of dark magic, and become more powerful than even the dark stars. Just wait and see, General. I will be the first King to lead the clowns into a new era of black magic."

13

The Battle of the Suns

Cabis stood at the door of Epsilon's chamber and knocked loudly.

"Come in. Ah, Cabis. What word do you bring from the heavens?"

"Epsilon, the most powerful suns of the thirteen heavens are mobilizing in the first heaven. They will attack our legions in the fourth quadrant that are preparing to attack the celestial palace."

Epsilon looked solemn and sat silently for a moment before he pounded his fist onto the wooden table.

"I must speak with Mancai. We will need additional forces to gather at once in order to defeat the army of the suns. I will call for you soon, Cabis."

Cabis bowed and left Epsilon alone in his chamber. Epsilon quickly rose to his feet and summoned his gateway to the heavens with a wave of his wand. He put on his black hooded cloak and touched the floating crystal orb. Epsilon shot through the gateway to the heavens faster than the speed of light, and arrived in the first heaven in the blink of an eye. He passed quickly through the first heaven and the black gateway of Zenith, then made his way to the Srilinaya Star Fields and landed in the cold frozen fields. He found his way to a cave carved out of ice located on the dead star Alpha Pegasi, and brushed away the frost that covered the star stone that controlled the gateway to the other heavens.

"Lord Perilous. Hear me and grant me entrance to your realm so that I may receive counsel from you, my Lord, and speak with my father Mancai."

A cold sweat formed on Epsilon's brow as he waited in the dark, cold cave.

"Lord Perilous, hear me, for I am the one that you have raised up to carry out your will throughout the thirteen heavens. I require an audience with Mancai and you."

Epsilon closed his eyes and gripped the cold star stone. He suddenly felt the stone begin to grow warmer under his palm, and he opened his eyes and saw the gateway opening. Epsilon walked through and instantly set foot on the dark planet. He began to walk across the land covered in molten rock as he used to do, and saw a figure in the distance moving towards him.

"Father, I am in urgent need of your wisdom," said Epsilon.

"Yes my son, Perilous told me that you called to him from the gateway and begged an audience with us. I have heard that the thirteen suns have gathered in the fourth quadrant of the first heaven and will march on the deylai forces gathered there," said Mancai.

"Yes, Father. We do not have the power to defeat them, and we must retreat and rebuild our forces in order to take the celestial palace."

"You do not have the power because you have grown weak, my son. Your heart is not truly devoted to the power of darkness. Fear and love are your mortal enemies, and create chaos in your mind."

"Father, I fear nothing and my love lies only in bringing the will of the forces of the dark to the heavens of light so that the heavens can finally be unified."

"I see your heart, Epsilon, and it is far from me. You would not be here out of doubt and fear if this were untrue. You would have rest assured in the knowledge that the power of darkness is greater than the power of all of the suns in the thirteen heavens combined. Your lack of faith disappoints me."

"The student mirrors the teacher, Father. We must be practical. Victory is ours, but only if we prepare."

"Is it up to me to teach you the ways of the dark forces yet again? I wish you were with me when I desolated Arokaya with my right hand. The same power is yours, my son, but your mind must be clear.

We will meet these thirteen suns in battle, and we will be victorious. Now go and prepare. We will march on the army of the suns very soon. I will meet you in the fourth quadrant when the moons of Haknami are just on the horizon of the vernal equinox."

Epsilon bowed low and began to journey back to the portal to the first heaven. Mancai watched his son walk away, and then turned to walk back to the fortress of the Demon Lord Perilous. He entered the grand room of the Demon Lord and found him feasting on the roasted legs of the fallen trolls—freshly harvested from the troll fields.

"I hope that he is now ready, Mancai. Were you able to persuade him?"

"Yes, my Lord. He will ready the deylai to march on the suns, but I will have to win this battle myself. He grows weak, my Lord, and I am afraid that he will not be able to carry out your will across the heavens. He still loves. I can sense it, and that love will be his downfall."

Lord Perilous ripped through a troll leg with his pointy teeth and wiped his mouth with his arm. He stopped to drink from his large gold chalice and then peered at Mancai with his red eyes.

"I trust that you will do what needs to be done, Mancai. I will hold you personally responsible if Epsilon fails to defeat the army of the suns."

"He will not fail, my Lord. I will strike them myself if I have to in order to ensure our victory," said Mancai.

"The celestial dragons have taken back Arokaya. We need this victory to demonstrate that we will not be defeated," said Perilous.

"Yes, my Lord. Now I must take leave and prepare. I will bring good news upon my return."

"Kun hanas rebat fiwrath. May you fight with the power of the wrath of fire."

Mancai bowed and exited the chamber of Perilous.

* * *

"Duchess, you have to stand strong with your feet apart when you strike with your sword. Like this, see."

General Sharaya raised her sword over her head and stood firm, swinging her sword back and forth.

"Now you and Thimble work together."

"Ouch, Duchess! You are swinging too hard. We're just practicing."

"I have to practice, Thimble. Sharaya let me try it with you, and Lez you go with Thimble," said Duchess.

Thimble rubbed her sore arm and pouted as she walked over to her sister Lez. Duchess faced Sharaya with a slight grin on her face and raised her sword. General Sharaya met her gaze and grinned. The two began to cross swords.

"Good, Duchess. Very good. You've been practicing. Now let's try something a bit more advanced. Follow my lead now and step with me. It's very much like a dance, you see. Good, good. Now lunge and attack. Again, lunge, lunge now attack and then feint. Good. Now try this with the wooden sword. It's called a kote-uchi. Watch me."

General Sharaya struck Duchess' wrist with a wooden sword and Duchess dropped hers.

"Ouch!"

"It wasn't that hard, Duchess. I could have done it harder. Now you try it on me."

Duchess tried to strike General Sharaya's wrist but the General moved too quickly.

"Try again, Duchess. Now step with me. There you go—good. Parry and then lunge. Step to the left and try to attack the wrist. Good, there you go. See? You disarmed me. Now do it again," said the General.

Duchess heard a familiar laugh over her shoulder and saw her father King Zionous attempting to help her sister Thimble with her sword fighting. His infectious laugh brought a smile to Duchess' face. The King looked over and saw that Duchess and Sharaya had stopped and walked over to them.

"Sharaya, I must speak with you. Let's walk down to the meadow and chat."

"Of course, Uncle. I could have come to you. You are a King Uncle. You can summon me," said General Sharaya.

King Zionous laughed.

"I'd rather be out here in the fresh air than locked up in that stuffy castle. I need to stretch my legs, and the fresh air helps me think. There is much that I must ponder."

General Sharaya placed the wooden training sword on the ground and began to walk with the King.

"I need you to journey to the fourth quadrant right away. Felanthiam has learned that Arev has gathered an army of the thirteen most powerful suns to attack Epsilon's forces, in opposition to the council's approval. King Ammon will accompany her and Commander Niran's unit to try and stop him. I'd like you to take a Fairish guardian squadron there and assist them. I am leaving for the celestial palace with a legion of soldiers tonight to assist in the defense of the celestial palace."

"Of course, my King. I will leave right away. Sire, with your permission, I would like to take Duchess with me. She has asked to accompany me on missions and I think she is ready. She wants to fight to defend her people and she should be given the chance to do so."

"She is not yet ready, Sharaya, and I will not risk losing her again."

"Your Highness, if war comes to Eucaron we will need all able-bodied fairies to fight. She will be more protected if she is ready before that time comes. I will not let anything happen to her. I will guard her with my life, I swear it."

* * *

"Your flying has much improved, Duchess. Soon you'll be able to start drilling battle formation attacks. Now stay close to me. Tensions are running high and if the deylai attack we must retreat to the celestial palace. I don't expect them to attack until Epsilon arrives, but we must be careful. I promised King Zionous that I would keep you safe."

Duchess and General Sharaya arrived at the fourth quadrant and saw that the meeting had already begun. The suns had taken human form and were each in a chariot of fire. Flames of black, blue, red and yellow burned brightly behind them. Felanthiam rode on the back of the King of the celestial dragons, King Ammon.

"Arev, pull back your forces at once. It is rumored that Mancai has come from the seventh heaven to destroy your armies. There are worlds that will die without the light of the sun. If you put yourself in harm's way you risk the lives of many," said Felanthiam.

"The council has failed us, Mother. These weak and ancient

celestials are not fit to decide our fates any longer. We must demonstrate our power to both Epsilon and Mancai, and stop this war before it even begins. No one can stop the power of the great suns! Even the sun of the twelfth heaven that burns with black flame joins us. This is an omen of our victory that is soon to come, mother," said Arev.

"Felanthiam, the deylai are attacking! You must retreat to the celestial palace!" Shouted General Sharaya.

Felanthiam turned and saw blue fire rising in the distance from the deylai's fleet of star flyers. King Ammon roared and immediately flew back towards the celestial palace with Felanthiam safely on his back. Commander Niran and his soldiers followed close behind them. General Sharaya grabbed Duchess' hand and flew at the rear of Commander Niran's unit to ensure there was no danger. Arev and the thirteen suns boldly turned and faced the deylai soldiers that advanced on them.

"Assume formation! My brothers and sisters, today we stand and fight to put an end to these dark forces that seek to desolate our worlds once and for all. We, the suns of our heavens, are the most powerful celestials on high and we cannot be defeated!" yelled Arev.

The thirteen suns roared in unison and charged into battle. Arev raised his triton made of star fire and vanquished one hundred deylai soldiers in a single swoop. The other suns followed his lead and raised their weapons that wielded the power of celestial flame, and overcame hundreds of deylai soldiers. The battle was quick, and the suns defeated an entire legion of soldiers. Arev and the thirteen suns cheered.

"We have beaten them! Now ride with me, my brethren, to

Gateway City, where we will bring Epsilon to his knees and end this war!" shouted Arev.

The thirteen suns turned and prepared to fly to Gateway City when they heard a voice that was carried on a strong solar wind surround them.

"You fools! You are all powerless against me! Pledge your allegiance to me and give me the star scroll of the burning suns and I will not annihilate you and your worlds. Choose this day whom you will serve."

A chariot of black flame started to speed towards them, and the power of the solar winds grew stronger and engulfed the thirteen suns. Mancai stopped his chariot when he reached them, and watched the black solar winds that he conjured with dark magic engulf the thirteen suns and render them powerless.

"We will not surrender to you, nor will we bow to your will!" Arev shouted as he struggled against the powerful winds.

"You will never defeat us!"

Mancai laughed.

"I have already defeated you. The great Arev will soon be nothing but ashes that are carried by the solar winds into the great abyss. If you do not surrender, then what use do I have for any of you?"

The thirteen suns shot star fire with their weapons, but nothing could penetrate the solar winds that engulfed them.

"Enough of this! I will reduce all of you to ash!"

Mancai raised his right hand and prepared to desolate them all, when the sun of the twelfth heaven cried out.

"Wait! Have mercy on me, great one. I surrender to you."

"Excellent, Matthias. I suggest you persuade the rest of

your brethren to follow in your footsteps."

Each of the suns began to surrender to Mancai until Arev was the only one left.

"You stand alone, Arev."

"You cowards! You will all pay for your treachery! I know who you are, dark one. I will never surrender to you, and I will never give you the scroll that you seek!"

"Good, Arev. Very good. I hoped that you would say that. I have plans for you and your power is very valuable to me. I will have the scroll of the burning suns by the time the demons of Haknami are done with you."

Mancai used his solar winds to bind Arev, and he pulled him from his chariot of fire and dragged him behind his chariot of black flame through the camp of the remaining deylai in the fourth quadrant. Arev saw legions of deylai soldiers ready to attack the celestial palace. *We are truly doomed,* he thought. *What power can defeat this vast army?*

14

The Rise of Mancai and the Capture of Kiranales

Felanthiam flew on the back of King Ammon, past the floating aquatic planetary system of Leinani in the aquanotic region of the third heaven. The journey to the realm of the Tanatoors that lay deep within the Cantarian galaxy was long. Yet, the King of the celestial dragons flew quickly with the mother of stars safely on his back.

"Fly with haste, Ammon. We have little time to waste. The deylai are at our door and will attack the palace at any moment."

"Your Majesty, I do not think it wise to have left the celestial palace. The deylai are advancing on the palace as we speak."

"We have no choice, Ammon. We must do what needs to be done. Time is short."

King Ammon roared and breathed a burst of celestial fire as he increased his speed and flew even faster than before. They soon touched down on the sole island in the region of the Theptums on the planet of Araxia. Felanthiam dismounted the celestial dragon, stepped onto the sandy beach and began to walk into the crystal clear water. The water felt cool against her warm skin. She noticed bubbles coming from under the water not too far from her. Three Theptum guardians rose out of the water and bowed to Felanthiam. Kiranales, Queen of the Theptums, was the last to appear. She swam quickly to Felanthiam and embraced her warmly.

"Felanthiam. It has been too long. I am sorry to visit with you again under these circumstances."

"Oh, my dear, I have missed you. I am sorry to hear of your father's death," said Felanthiam.

"Thank you, Felanthiam. He was blessed to live a long life and lead our people to a new home here on Araxia. I know that time is of the essence. Let us depart for the region of the Tanatoors immediately," said Kiranales.

With that, Felanthiam made her way back to the beach and mounted King Ammon's back. Queen Kiranales and her Theptum guardians rose from the water surrounded in flying water capsules, and they all lifted into the sky and began to fly to the realm of the Tanatoors. They flew quickly to the other side of the Araxian world, and touched down on the lone island of Avantarus where the Tanatoors often meet with beings from other worlds. The small island was quiet, and the palm trees swayed slowly in the calm breeze. King Ammon breathed heavily and stood at attention.

"Steady, Ammon. The Tanatoors will not harm us."

Felanthiam dismounted and patted King Ammon's scaly leg. The sea grew more restless, and large waves began to crash against the beach. Large figures started to appear in the shallow water, and the mighty Kings and Lords of the Cantarian Tanatoors rose out of the water.

"King Halan. It is good to see you, my friend," said Felanthiam.

"My Queen. It is good to see you in dark times such as these. Your presence here brings us great comfort. I have brought my advisors with me to help persuade Kano and his people to join the high celestials."

"You are all welcome here. Queen Kiranales has agreed to come and speak as our advocate. I only hope that Kano and his people will listen to reason."

The waves crashed on the other side of the small island, and the Simeonic Tanatoors rose slowly from the water one giant tentacle at a time. Felanthiam, Kiranales and all of the Tanatoors gathered in the shallow water and quietly waited for Felanthiam to speak.

"My friends, thank you for gathering here in our time of need. We do not live in times of peace, but of darkness. The heavens of light are under siege and those who seek war with us desire to destroy not only our physical beings, but the essence of light from which we were born. It grieves me to say that the fate of Arokaya is not far from all of us that dwell in the first heaven.

We must bond together as one this very day. Mancai has returned with the blessings of the Lords of the black heavens. We thought that Epsilon was a threat to us, but now we realize that the situation is far more dire with the union of the dark heavens. We ask that you stand with us to defend the celestial palace and fight this war. If Mancai and his forces capture the palace all will be lost."

"Why should we side with the high celestials of the first heaven when they did nothing for Milandria when Arokaya was reduced to ash? It was Mancai that humbled us, and we will pay tribute to his son Epsilon. It is the only way that our people will survive this war!"

King Kano's tentacles wriggled angrily as he spoke, and his council cheered in agreement. Queen Kiranales swam into the center of the gathering and motioned for the Tanatoors to be quiet.

"King Kano, my people and I were there alongside the Tanatoors when Milandria was destroyed, and our entire universe was turned into a wasteland. Without the aid of the high celestials, we would have died with our old world. It's the high celestial army that held back Mancai and his forces long enough for us to escape. Is it in our customs to repay kindness with disloyalty?"

"Kano, we fought alongside each other in the wars of old. Don't let fear be your guide. We must stand united," said King Halan.

"You are one to talk, Halan. It was my people that were on the front lines and the first to be slaughtered, not yours," said King Kano with venomous disdain.

The Tanatoors erupted into a ferocious argument, and Felanthiam did her best to silence them. King Ammon let out a loud roar that shook the tiny island, and the Tanatoors finally fell silent.

"My brothers and sisters. We are all of one flesh. We will stand as one, fight as one and fall as one body. No life here is worth more than another. When Mancai came the first time to Milandria, Erog gave her life to save our people. The high celestials sacrificed the lives of many to spare ours. It is time that we are willing to do the same for the survival of our people. Kano, will you stand with us?" asked Kiranales.

The Tanatoors all fell silent. The sound of the waves crashing on the beach was ear shattering amid the dead silence. King Kano adjusted his crown with his large tentacles and turned to speak with his advisers. After a few moments, King Kano turned to face Felanthaim, Kiranales, and his fellow Tanatoors.

"After speaking with my advisers, I have decided that my people and I will stand with you all in the fight against the dark stars. You have been successful in your plea, Queen Kiranales. I will gather my finest warriors and we will journey to the celestial palace at once."

"We are truly grateful, King Kano. Commander Niran will rendezvous with the Tanatoors and lead the march to the celestial palace. Go in peace, all of you," said Felanthiam.

All of the Tanatoors that gathered there said farewell, descended into the water peacefully and soon disappeared into the deepest parts of the ocean.

* * *

"How could you let this happen, Epsilon! You have been far too diplomatic with the Tanatoors, and now we've lost them to the high celestials. Instead of giving them gifts you should have ruled them by fear! I hope that you now know what you must do, my son. You must kill Kiranales. I will say no more," said Mancai.

Mancai turned quickly and left Epsilon standing alone in his tower. He picked up his vials full of potions and threw them against the wall in anger. The potions crashed against the wall, and black smoke from their remnants evaporated into the air. Epsilon felt like his throat was starting to close, and he stumbled onto his balcony, gasping for air. Falling to his knees, he screamed into the dark sky. Tears fell from his eyes, and he shut them tightly. The memory of his beloved Kiranales floated into his mind. Epsilon gripped his hair with both hands and tried hard to forget her face. He sprang to his feet, searched for the ancient book of the star of Andeeri and quickly found the words that had brought him comfort many times before.

"To us who are righteous, may we always do what we are called to do so that the union of the heavens will be ruled by the one true force in all thirteen heavens that is the darkness."

Epsilon closed the book and held it to his chest.

"Iona Draconis, hear me and give me the strength to do what I must do for us who have fallen from on high."

Epsilon breathed a sigh of relief and quickly summoned the gateway to the heavens. The crystal orb that would transport him to the heavens appeared in the center of the room and Epsilon was off to the planet of Araxia. He landed on the small island of

Avantarus and planned to use an incantation to find Kiranales. He touched his hand to the ground, closed his eyes and whispered an incantation into the wind.

She has been here. I feel her essence. He thought.

Epsilon flew quickly across Araxia to the realm of the Theptums and transformed into Theptum form as he dove into the clear, turquoise-colored water. He swam quickly to the palace and found Queen Kiranales unguarded in her courtyard, tending to her garden of sea coral.

"The Tanatoors saw your light as you flew in and informed me of your arrival. You were never able to surprise me, were you Epsilon?"

Kiranales turned and looked at him, and gasped at his appearance.

"You are not the Epsilon that I once knew and loved. Dark magic has made you into a creature of the night," said Kiranales.

Epsilon stood still and tried to remember the words written in the book of Andeeri, but could see nothing and could think of nothing other than the beauty that was before him.

"Your face...it haunts me in my dreams. I still remember who we were and how much you meant to me.

"Epsilon, it's not too late for you. You can stop this war from taking even more lives. Join us and Felanthiam will welcome you back into the heavens with open arms."

"You know why I have come, Kiranales. Mancai has sent me here to take your life. I must do it, or he will take mine. I have no other choice."

Kiranales screamed for her guards, but by the time they arrived, she was gone.

Kiranales struggled to break free from Epsilon's grip while he swam furiously through the waters of Araxia.

"Epsilon, let me go! You don't know what you're doing! Take me back, and the waters of Erog can heal you."

"There is no turning back for me now. The blackness of the deep has taken me, and I must give in to it, I must. Your love binds me—controls my every thought. I must be free of you, and rule with the hand of darkness. This is my destiny!"

"Mancai has lied to you Epsilon. Your destiny is in your own hands. It's not too late to turn back now. Look, the waters of Erog flow from the Causilic just ahead."

"I will not yield to your lies! You must die!"

"Watch out!"

Theptum guardians swam quickly towards them and fired upon Epsilon. He was struck by a tri-spear and instantly released Kiranales from his grasp. His injured body started to fall to the bottom of the ocean, but Kiranales caught him in her arms.

"Stop! Ceasefire! Epsilon can you hear me? Quickly, take him to the Causilic and put him on the altar."

Kiranales and her Theptum guardians swam with Epsilon to the Causilic and placed him on the altar. Kiranales put her hands on his face and looked deeply into his dark eyes.

"Epsilon, can you hear me? Speak to me, please. May the waters of Erog surround you and heal you. Listen to my voice, my love. What does your heart say that you are? Hold on to the light that I know is still inside you."

The waters that flowed from the statue of Erog flowed around Epsilon and into his wounds as he gasped for air.

Kiranales closed her eyes and prayed to the waters.

"Return to me, my love. I beg you."

Silence surrounded them for a long moment. Only the sound of gently flowing water could be heard until Epsilon spoke.

"I'll never leave you, my dear."

"Epsilon! Thanks to the waters and Erog in all her grace! I thought that I'd lost you. I can see your kind heart through your eyes once again. The celestial that I fell in love with has returned."

Epsilon slowly sat up with the help of Kiranales and peered at his reflection in the water.

"I never thought that I would see the natural color of my eyes ever again."

Epsilon turned and embraced Kiranales.

"I heard them Nales, the waters. They spoke to me. I do not yet know my destiny, but I see now that the way of darkness can no longer be my path. Your love that has lasted through the ages of space and time has made me see the light, and I must remain here. There is much more that I must learn and do to make amends for all that I've done."

* * *

Mancai walked down the corridor of the royal clown palace and entered the throne room.

"What is this? Who are you, and what right have you to barge in here? Guards seize him!" said Jax.

The clown guards stood still and seemed to be unable to move or speak. Jax stood stunned and speechless at the stranger that had just paraded into his throne room and paralyzed his guards. Jax steadied his nerves and calmly took his seat.

"I assume you to be a dark star. Or are you some other dark creature sent here by Epsilon? What business do you have here? Speak, I say!"

"Epsilon has betrayed us, and he will soon be no more. I've come here in person to retrieve the scroll of the kingdom of witches. If you stand with me as you did with Epsilon then prepare your troops, for war is upon this kingdom. Once I take the celestial palace, the entire universe will soon be under my control, and your troops must advance quickly. If you choose to fight with the humans against me, then you will perish with them."

Jax stood still as he looked upon the stranger that had just entered his presence so arrogantly. Epsilon was powerful in appearance and stature, but Mancai seemed to be an ancient cryptic evil from another place and time.

"The alliance between my house and Epsilon has gone back many years. Epsilon was a powerful sorcerer, but he needed my father, and my father needed him when he was alive. I assume that this is no longer the case? Also, what is your name?" Asked Jax.

Mancai turned to leave without answering Jax's question.

"I am not known in this present time. My power has never been unleashed in this heaven, but soon all will know my name. I am Mancai."

As soon as the words left Mancai's mouth, Jax heard his footsteps echo in the royal corridor, and he was out of sight. Jax's heart was pounding. He quickly stepped out onto his balcony to catch his breath. General Madix and the members of his Royal Clown Guard ran in seconds later.

"Yer majesty, we was rendered powerless by the dark star. We couldn't move nor speak," said General Madix panting breathlessly.

"We have no power over the dark stars, General. We must prove ourselves valuable to them until we find our own source of power that will defeat them and anyone that tries to rule over us. How are the magicians coming along in their studies?"

"Their work is slow, yer highness, but they seem to be pro-gressin' their powers." Said General Madix.

"That's good, but it may not be soon enough. I want you to send guardsmen to seize their families and imprison all of them until the new magical system is powerful enough to overtake the dark stars. Janice must lead this expedition. Since she continues to refuse to be of use, then she can work with the magicians."

"As yeh command yer Highness."

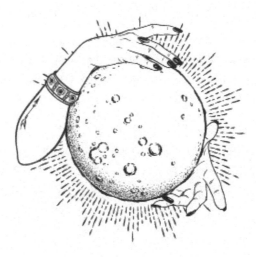

15

The 2nd Coming of Vangemtra

Lyanthra was a planet deep within the twelfth heaven where darkness first rested. In the time before celestial rule, the spirit Lords of the thirteen realms ruled each heaven. Lord Ranis built his empire in this world and collected lost souls for his amusement. The planet became the home of death and black flame, and Lord Ranis was confined by the celestials to Lyanthra to care for only the dark souls that had yet to find rest.

Mancai flew high over Lyanthra. He could hear the souls below moaning in anguish as he flew closer to the surface. Mancai often flew to Lyanthra to seek the counsel of the spirit of Ranis. The souls that dwelled there became one with the earth that was covered in black tar. The souls cried out day and night wanting to be released, and telling of the dark prophetic murmurs of the forces of shadow that gathered there. Faces appeared from time to time in the tar that pierced the darkness and spoke of things of old and things yet to come.

On this night, the souls seemed more excited than usual. White eyes and hands erupted from the tar that covered Lyanthra and flowed below, trying to break free. Tarred hands shot out from the tar and desperately reached for Mancai. Some of the most powerful of the dark souls took the form of tar people and stumbled about the dark planet, craving freedom before being pulled back into the earth by Ranis' slaves. Mancai ascended onto the volcanic mountain that was the high place where Ranis dwelt, and bowed low before the shadow that surrounded the mountain.

"To the Lord of darkness that was here before the stars were born, I beg for your wisdom and to rule one day as you once ruled the twelfth heaven. It was foretold down in the dark. Yes, here in the tar pits of Lyanthra the future was seen. This is where the great witch ruler Vangemtra went after she died in the great war of old. I still remember that dark day, but the souls of Lyanthra have given us hope and have foretold that she will rise again on the night of the thirteen suns.

I see my beautiful child once again upon the black throne of the kingdom of witches. When she rises, she will rule with the power of the night forevermore. The words of the prophecy of the thirteen suns have been etched into stone in the language of the underworld that only they who belong know. This stone was fashioned in the flames of Lyanthra, and I myself fastened the tablet above the throne of Witch Kingdom. Lord Ranis, now is the time for my child to rise again. Her brother has betrayed us, and I am in need of her to help me carry on your will."

The mountain shook as the dark shadow engulfed it.

"You know the price, Mancai! She has failed to pay for her return to the living with 10,000 souls, and it is before her time!"

Mancai shook with fear at the voice of Ranis. It was menacing and black like the voice of the very darkness itself.

"My Lord, you are right and true in all that you say. Today is the day that the thirteen suns have been defeated and the prophecy has been fulfilled. I have also brought you a gift. It is the ancient book of the star of Andeeri. I bring this as payment for my beloved Vangemtra."

The shadow began to shriek as if in pain.

"Where did you find this? It has been lost to the darkness for centuries."

"Yes, indeed it has, my Lord. The old Wiseman Polus kept it from us, and now I have returned it to you, its rightful owner."

"Place it upon the altar. Let me feel its power. The great creator of the dark, Iona Draconis, spoke to the star of Andeeri and filled her with the spirit of the night to write this ancient book so that all may understand that light does not exist without darkness. It is of great importance to the dark realm, and its words shall bring me comfort."

"It brings me great joy to hear of this, my Lord. It is also the day that the thirteen suns have been defeated, great one. Let the prophecy of the dead souls be fulfilled, and let Vangemtra live again," said Mancai.

The dark shadow of Ranis consumed the book of the star

of Andeeri and murmured prayers in the ancient tongue of the underworld. Mancai sat on the hot earth and closed his eyes. The spirits below began to chant with Ranis, and the melodic sound brought comfort to him. After the ceremony was completed Ranis finally spoke.

"So let it be done," said Ranis.

The sound of rushing wind filled the mountaintop, and the pool of black tar that lay under the altar began to swirl. The swirling tar grew taller and taller until it formed the shape of a human. The being wailed as it transformed into the once power-ful sorceress, Vangemtra. Mancai ran and caught his daughter in his hands. She breathed heavily and coughed up black tar.

"My child, you are weak from the transformation. Rest for a moment, then I will take you to Haknami to recover."

Vangemtra's eyes were still black with tar, and she gasped for air.

"Father...Father. I've missed your voice. Without you, I would be wriggling around in these wretched tar pits."

"My daughter, I would never abandon your soul to be lost for an eternity here on Lyanthra. War is upon us, and time is short. I must get you to Haknami."

"What has happened, Father, and where is Epsilon? Is he well?"

"Epsilon will soon be no more. He has abandoned his faith and betrayed us to the high celestials, but I will attack the celes-tial palace on this night, and the first heaven will soon be ours."

"Let me come with you, Father. I will stand by your side and fight. My strength grows with every passing moment."

"If your strength grows then make your way to Witch

Kingdom. Nothing will get in my way of taking the celestial palace. You must find the thirteenth scroll and unlock it. This will unleash the power of all the star scrolls combined."

"I will not disappoint you, Father. Leave the thirteenth scroll to me. I will seek out the Twills and make them give it to me. If anyone in the universe knows where it is, the Twills surely do."

"Seek out Loxidor. I hear that he has found the hidden home of the Twills, and the scrolls that they protect."

* * *

Vangemtra felt her strength begin to return with every tilt of her broom. She flew through the dark skies with speed, despite her weakened state. The thick air seemed to energize her, and she was finally able to see Witch Kingdom in the distance. Vangemtra cackled loudly and increased her speed. She landed in the courtyard of the ancient palace and opened the doors with a simple wave of her hand. The old castle was dark and abandoned. Its deteriorated state indicated that not one soul had set foot inside of it in centuries. Vangemtra gazed upon the grand black caldron that was in the center of her throne room and thought of the fire dances that the witches had there many years ago.

Vangemtra closed her eyes and touched the caldron. She spoke an incantation, and fire appeared under the caldron. The entire throne room lit up. She smiled as she walked down the lit hallway and watched the cobwebs and dust disappear from the words of her spell. *These tattered robes will not do. I must return to my former glory. They will all know once again the name of the Ancient Supreme Sorceress, Vangemtra.* She gazed at her wardrobe and watched the dust and moths melt away. Vangemtra picked up a purple satin gown and quickly put it on. *That's much better.* She thought.

The sound of horses flooding the courtyard brought a smile to her face, and she hurried back into the great hall and sat upon her black throne. Knights, witches, and sorcerers in fine robes burst through the doors and approached the great black throne.

"Great one, we were all awaiting your return in the field of the harvest moon. The prophecy has been fulfilled, and the great Lord Ranis has returned you to us. I am Mercuriel, of the House of Grimorie, and we are your humble servants."

Vangemtra gazed upon her humble subjects and smiled.

"Grimorie. Masca Grimorie? He served faithfully as my second in command in the great wars of old. He was a powerful warlock, and his house will always be welcome in my great hall. We are on the brink of war, my brethren, and I must be able to spy on my enemies as I used to. I must rest and visit the methelum pools."

"Of course, my Queen. The high priests have made a sacrifice just this night so that you may have sight into all that you wish to see."

"Excellent. I will be able to regain much of my strength in our holy place. I must use the methelum pools to search for Loxidor and meet with him. He will know how to find the remaining star scrolls."

"Yes, my Queen. We will accompany you to the temple."

Mercuriel rose from his knees and offered his arm to Vangemtra. She grasped it and pulled herself to her feet.

Mercuriel helped her into the carriage that waited for them in the courtyard, and the horses galloped quickly towards the temple of Iona Draconis.

The journey to the temple of Iona Draconis was long. The temple sat on top of the mountain of druids, and the high altar lay in its center. Mercuriel whispered a spell under his breath to keep Vangemtra's strength from failing during their travels. They finally arrived at the temple and the druid priests ran quickly to meet them.

"The souls of Lyanthra told us that Vangemtra had risen. Come, we must get her into the pools."

The priests carried Vangemtra into the largest methelum pool in the temple and laid her in it. Mercuriel tried to follow, but the druids would not let him enter the temple.

"Only the chosen may enter the temple of Draconis. You must wait here unless you are called. She is healing, and she will soon be more powerful than she was before."

Vangemtra felt her strength starting to return as soon as the water surrounded her. The sound of the druids whispering incantations brought her peace. She began to use the healing waters to search for Loxidor in her mind. The temple high priest walked slowly towards the methelum pool where she lay and knelt beside her.

"My Queen, you must rest."

"Masca, is that you? I know your voice, my friend. I see that Iona Draconis has granted you the gift of immortality to serve as high priest here. I need your help, Masca. Help me find him. He is the key to the scrolls."

"Lay here another minute and then we will walk among the other pools. Iona Draconis often requires that we labor to find what we seek to honor the blood sacrifice that gives us our sight."

"Yes, Masca. It is clear to see why our great Iona Draconis has chosen you. Your House has become the most powerful in all the land, and Mercuriel leads them. Why have you not called him?"

"In time, my Queen. Everything must happen in its own time. Come, you are ready."

Masca helped Vangemtra to her feet, and they began to walk among the other methelum pools of water and blood that flowed from the altar.

"I sense that Loxidor is in this universe, but it's unclear to me if he is in this world. Do you remember how we used to walk for miles and miles among the pools during the old wars, Masca? We would come away from here with battle plans that annihilated our enemies," said Vangemtra.

"And so it will be again, my Queen.

I sense him here...There he is. In a place called Normandeery."

"Yes, I see him there too. Your power of sight has always been greater than mine, dear friend. I must leave at once."

Masca turned and looked at Vangemtra.

"The victory is yours, Vangemtra, whether you leave now or later. Walk among the pools and pay homage to our great Draconis, then be on your way. Death has made you stronger, and you will be more powerful than you have ever been before."

Mercuriel tried not to let his rage show in the holy place of Draconis. He waited for what seemed like an eternity before he finally saw Vangemtra emerge from the temple.

"My Queen, I am grateful that the waters have restored your strength."

"Mercuriel, you've waited all this time? Your loyalty to the crown brings me great joy. I'd like your knights and you to be part of my wiccen fighters and accompany me to Normandeery."

"Your wish is my command, my Queen. My house and I are your humble servants. I wish one day to be worthy of being called to this high place to experience the great spirit of Iona Draconis."

"Yes, Mercuriel. You must be patient. Everything must happen in its own time. We must leave at once. We will fly in formation as we used to do in the old days," said Vangemtra.

Vangemtra and Mercuriel walked into the temple courtyard and met the Knights of Grimorie. The druids handed them their brooms, and they all lifted into the sky as soon as they mounted them.

* * *

Normandeery was a hidden land that was protected by celestial magic. When Vangemtra, Mercuriel and the Knights of Grimorie arrived, all they could see was fog.

"They must be here somewhere...We must find a way through the fog. Do not break formation," Vangemtra commanded.

Vangemtra and her fighters flew into the fog, but couldn't find a way through. The more they tried to find a way out, the thicker the mist grew.

"Vangemtra, look. Loxidor and his trolls have found a way into Normandeery."

Vangemtra turned and saw the fog beginning to clear where Loxidor and his trolls were gathered on the ground. Vangemtra flew quickly to where they were, and where Loxidor had broken through the fog with his imperial staff. Loxidor and his troll warriors rushed through the fog and began to attempt an assault on the tiny village below, but their arrows could not penetrate the magical boundary.

"Loxidor, your weapons are useless against celestial magic. We must break the barrier with dark magic."

Loxidor raised his hand and signaled his archers to hold their fire. Vangemtra, Mercuriel and the Knights of Grimorie raised their hands and began to speak incantations over the magical barrier that protected Normandeery. Their eyes turned black as their voices grew louder. The transparent barrier cracked loudly, and the Twills of Normandeery started to emerge from their huts. The small Twills took formation and prepared to fight the trolls and witches with nothing more than their wooden staffs. The magical barrier continued to crack until the holes were large enough for troll warriors to get through.

The Twills fought bravely and with more fierceness than even the witches anticipated. They battled with their wooden staffs and were able to stop some of the most colossal troll warriors that were sent through the barrier. As the witches incantations continued, the barrier crumbled more and more until hordes of troll warriors were able to break through. There were simply too many for the small Twills to fight, and Twills began to be killed or captured. The remaining pieces of the magical barrier came crashing down, and the witches started their aerial assault.

"Mercuriel, take five of your knights and seek out the library. The Twills will be hiding the remaining scrolls of light there," commanded Vangemtra.

"Yes, my Queen."

Mercuriel and his knights flew swiftly to the center of the village and touched down in front of a massive building made of marble. They stormed in and found Twills in white togas standing ready to fight. One of them stepped forward and raised his staff towards Mercuriel.

"We expel you from this place, sorcerer! We are the ordained protectors of the celestial scrolls, and we will shed our blood before letting any dark magic into this place!"

"So be it, Twill."

Mercuriel raised his hands and began chanting in the ancient language of Lyanthra. The master of Twills that stepped forward was instantly vanquished, and his ashes flew into the wind that swept through Normandeery. The other Twills began to attack immediately.

"Don't kill them all. Leave some alive for questioning. Master Druix is in need of some new pets for his collection. I will look for the scrolls," said Mercuriel.

The Knights of the House Grimorie fought the remaining Twills while Mercuriel stepped calmly into the library. Scrolls were stacked on shelves from ground to ceiling. Mercuriel stood in the center of the library and closed his eyes. He began to search for the scrolls of light in his mind. The room began to shake and the scrolls began to fall from the shelves. A hidden door was revealed on the north wall once the scrolls had fallen to the ground.

"Mercuriel, the Twills have been beaten. We have left four alive," said the Captain of Guard.

"Good. Bring them here to me," said Mercuriel.

The Knights of the House Grimorie fought the remaining Twills while Mercuriel stepped calmly into the library. Scrolls were stacked on shelves from the ground to the ceiling. Mercuriel stood in the center of the library and closed his eyes. He searched for the scrolls of light in his mind and used his powers to search every corner of the library. The room shook, and the scrolls fell from the shelves. A hidden door was revealed on the north wall once all the scrolls had fallen to the ground.

"Mercuriel, the Twills have been beaten. We have left four alive," said his Captain of the Grimorian Knights.

"Good. Bring them here to me," said Mercuriel.

The Knights of Grimorie brought the remaining Twills to him and made them kneel.

"I am Mercuriel of the most powerful House in Witch Kingdom, the House Grimorie; descendant of the eternal Masca Grimorie and right hand of the ancient supreme sorceress, Queen Vangemtra Eridani. I vanquished your master, and I bear the power granted to me from the all-powerful darkness, Iona Draconis, to vanquish any of you. You are all alive to serve as pets of our Dungeon Master, and we only desire to keep one of you. The first one that tells me how to open this door shall be spared."

The Twills all sat silently and began to hum the same tune

under their breath in unison.

"What are you singing, you street rats! Do you not understand what I'm saying to you? Tell me how to open this door!"

The Twills began to sing louder and louder.

"Love indeed will always be,
The better way to remedy,
A world that's built on pain and rage,
In a time that we've been left to pay.
The price of freedom for it all,
Makes what we do quite worth the fall."

Vangemtra entered the library and observed what was happening.

"Enough of this, Mercuriel. Knights, take the remaining Twills to Witch Kingdom, and I will burn this place to the ground. I guarantee that the star scrolls are buried underground. We don't need anything on this floor," said Vangemtra.

"Vangemtra, I hope that you are not disappointed in me. I was simply trying to find the scrolls and fulfill your wishes."

"Next time skip the dramatics, Mercuriel. There is much to be done. I will use the fire of the heart of Draconis to purify this place and bring the hidden places to our sight."

The knights quickly dragged the Twills out, and the library was empty. Vangemtra spoke the incantation of the heart of Draconis, and blue flames instantly lit the library on fire. Vangemtra and Mercurial stood amidst the flames unburned. The hidden door flew open, and Vangemtra and Mercuriel walked through the door and down into the crypt while the library burned. The dim light from torches flickered against the walls. In the center of the crypt was a crystal case with three scrolls. An old Twill was on his knees by the case praying. Vangemtra's eyes filled with tears.

"Finally. After all of this time, Mercuriel, we are so close to being one. Imagine the heavens all unified and returned to darkness as it was in the beginning."

"Here lies the scroll of Orion, The scroll of Rigil and the scroll of Felanthiam and the Celestial Dragons. I have protected these scrolls with my life, and now my life has to come to an end," said the old Twill.

"Your life will not be in vain old one. Mercuriel, see that this Twill is taken to the temple. Our blood sacrifices die without fear and pain. You will spend your last days there and be well. Your shed blood will flow from the altar of Iona Draconis and will be used to heal and provide foresight and wisdom to the noblest of witches. I will take these scrolls to my father, Mancai. After the armies of the fallen stars wage war on the celestial palace, we shall have the final scroll of light, the Arokayan scroll of the Centauries."

16

The Siege of the Celestial Palace

Felanthiam sat on the back of King Ammon and looked upon her troops gathered on the great wall of the celestial palace. Prince Proxima Centauri's three-headed gold dragon stood at attention next to King Ammon–anxiously awaiting the battle that was soon to come. King Augustus patted his fierce Eucrackian rock dragon made of black onyx that stood to the right of King Ammon and Felanthiam at the highest point of the castle. There they could see the army of the dark stars in formation in the distance.

"The soldiers have already toasted our victory, Sister," said Augustus.

"Don't be a fool, Augustus. Victory is never a simple task. Defeat is at our doorstep against such a power as Mancai. He holds the power of Iona Draconis in his hands," said Felanthiam.

"Epsilon has been of great help to us, Sister. I have confidence that we have what we need to defeat Mancai for good."

"Yes, that is if what he says is true and he doesn't betray us. He can't be trusted, Augustus. Proxima, the Arokayan star scroll is safe yes?" asked Felanthiam.

"Yes, Felanthiam. My second in command and his unit is guarding it within the celestial palace," said Proxima.

"Hopefully that will be enough to keep it safe. If Mancai retrieves the last scroll of light, our world as we know it will be plunged into darkness. Commander Niran, are all of our fighters in formation?"

Commander Niran bowed low before Felanthiam after he descended his white lion made of bright crystal flame.

"Yes, my Queen. The Tanatoors and Theptums will also be launching an assault on the deylai starting from the second star quadrant. They will be our first line of defense. Captain Naman and the Tanatoorian pirates will defend the first quadrant along with General Sharaya and the Fairish legions. Our high celestial guard will defend the wall and launch an aerial assault over the palace. King Zionous and his troops will defend the rear of the castle, but there really is no need since the castle sits on the edge of the Abisynian star field. We are fully protected in the rear, but King Zionous and Proxima's unit hold a line of defense at the tower in the rear of the castle."

"Excellent work, Commander. I don't know what I

would do without you by my side these many millennia," said Felanthiam.

"It has been my honor to fight at your side once again, my Queen," said Commander Niran.

The sound of deylai star flyers began to fill the air, and the Royals could see star fire light up the sky in the second quadrant.

* * *

Measles ducked his head, and a ball of black star fire flew over him and landed on the wooden deck of the Tanatoorian pirate ship that sailed through space. Captain Naman cheered as he spun the wheel of the ship wildly. The creaky boat swerved and dipped as it did its best to avoid fireballs being launched by the deylai.

"Man yer cannons, gents, an' fire at will! Let's show these blaggards what we pirates are made of!" Captain Naman yelled.

The pirate crew scrambled to their feet and began to refill the cannons and fire at will. Measles and Popcorn tried their best to keep up.

"Come on, Pop. Keep up now. I see one comin'. Hit that one, Pop."

Popcorn aimed his cannon at a deylai star flying straight towards the ship and fired.

"Blazin' dragon a plenty, Pop, yeh get 'em! Good aim, me boy. Yer really gettin' quite the hang o' this."

"You try one now, Meas. It's quite the good time. There's a big one right over there."

Measles huffed and puffed while he loaded a massive cannonball into the cannon. He shifted the cannon slightly to the left and fired.

"Yippee! Good aim, Meas! Yeh got 'im right smack dab in the kisser. Eh Cap, watch out fer the Tanatoor squadron comin' up now!"

Captain Naman spun the wheel of the ship hard to the right to avoid the massive creatures in flying water capsules that were floating through space. The squadron of Cantarian Tanatoors spewed poison from their stingers and ripped apart any deylai soldier that they could get their hands on.

"That was close, boys! The Tanatoors an' Theptums are bein' pushed back from the second quadrant. This is our fight now. We must defend the celestial palace!" shouted captain Naman.

The pirates all cheered in unison. Those that didn't man the cannons drew their swords and swung from the sails to fight the deylai star flyers. The forces of the fallen stars blackened the sky around them and the pirate ship was smothered in smoke and ash. Measles coughed and grabbed for his handkerchief.

"Pop, quick. Tie yer hanky around yer nose an' mouth. It'll keep this blasted smoke an' ash out."

Popcorn struggled to keep from coughing, and couldn't seem to find his handkerchief. He fell to the ground and Measles ran to his side. Measles tore a piece of cloth from his shirt and tied it around Popcorn's face.

"There yeh go friend. Look, Pop, yeh see those their flashes of light? The fairies be comin' fer us."

* * *

"Guardians! Right now is what is before us and what we

have been freely given. Today we stand together as one to protect all that has made us who we are and has given us light and breath in our bodies. Today we say to the darkness, 'You will not take us!' Today we say to the darkness, 'You will not win!' Today we will not run and hide, but we will fight—for today we become who we are, and we abandon our faults. Today is our time to shine in glory!"

The Fairish legions roared with loud voices at the words of General Sharaya. With wands raised, they marched into the ash and shadow and began to attack the deylai star flyers in the second quadrant.

"Duchess, go and tell Captain Naman to fall back to the celestial palace. There is nothing more that he can do here. And be careful!"

"Yes, General. Please be safe as well," said Duchess.

"I will, and we will toast our victory at the celestial palace. Now go quickly."

Duchess flew speedily through the smoke and ash, firing her wand at the deylai to clear a path. She spotted the pirate ship through the smoke and landed onboard.

"Captain Naman!" she yelled.

She covered her mouth with her arm to prevent the smoke from entering her lungs.

"Up there—he's up there!" she heard someone yell.

Duchess ran up the wooden stairs to the deck of the ship and spotted a very disheveled looking pirate Captain yelling furiously at his crew.

"Put out that fire, yeh lazy blaggarts. Fire those cannons an' don't yeh dare stop until we vanquish the lot of 'em, yeh mangy rats. The fairies are 'ere, gents. It won't be long now. Who in all blazes might you be?"

Captain Naman looked right at Duchess amid shouting orders and spinning the wheel of the ship in violent spurts.

"Captain Naman, General Sharaya sent me to tell you to fall back to the celestial palace."

Captain Naman spat on the ground and laughed loudly.

"Did yeh hear that, gents? We be called to the castle. Hold on to yer skivvies, boys. Hoist the mainsail. We be hard to starboard, gents, an' 'ere we go!"

Captain Naman spun the wheel of the ship furiously, and the ship made a sharp turn. The remaining crew held onto anything that they could to prevent themselves from flying off the ship. The boat creaked as it turned on its side and started to move forward speedily towards the celestial castle.

"Ha! That's me girl. Not too bad fer an old sea ship like she is, eh fairy?" said Captain Naman with a quick look over his shoulder at Duchess.

The farther that the ship traveled from the first quadrant, the more the smoke began to clear. Duchess was grateful that she could breathe again, but looked back to the battleground full of worry.

Stay safe, cousin, and may the stars watch over you, she prayed quietly.

The massive gates of the celestial palace opened, and the pirate ship sailed smoothly through and landed in the center of the courtyard. Duchess flew above the castle to search for her father. She saw him by Felanthiam's side at the highest point of the palace.

"Duchess, what are you doing here? You should not have come. I told you to stay on Eucharon," said King Zionous.

"I will not let the ones I love die in battle, Father. I want to fight to protect my family like Sharaya and you."

"You are a foolish girl. The same fierce stubbornness and courage as your mother. Stay by my side, and do as I tell you to do. I will keep you safe."

"Yes, Father. The Tanatoorian pirates have arrived and will help defend the castle. I fear that the deylai forces will not be defeated before making it to the wall."

"Indeed, my dear. We are ready to stand and fight for what is true to our hearts. What we have forged since light entered the world will not be easily taken from us."

The dragon King Ammon roared in despair and shuffled his feet.

"I cannot sit and watch any longer. King Ammon and I will try to take out any deylai that attempt to pass the first quadrant, before they are at our gates. Niran, Augustus, will you fly beside me?" Asked Felanthiam.

"Always and forever," Commander Niran said with a bow.

"Of course, Sister," said Augustus.

"I am grateful for both of you. Proxima, fly high above and protect the castle," said Felanthiam.

King Ammon roared and shot into the sky. The flames of the dragon and the mother of all stars were in unison as they flew to the first quadrant with Commander Niran and King Augustus at their sides.

Felanthiam arrived to the battlefield, and King Ammon consumed a fleet of deylai with just one breath of his celestial star fire. Felanthiam raised her sword and obliterated the dark stars that attacked her. The great rock dragon Matthias rode bravely into battle with King Augustus on his back and swung his mighty tail that toppled the deylai from their star flyers.

"Sister, we are victorious! You see, the deylai are no match for us. We've just defeated hundreds of them."

"Yes, Brother, but look at how many fairies, Theptums and Tanatoors have fallen. We cannot hold this quadrant any longer. The real battle begins when Mancai reveals himself."

Just then a chariot of black flame was seen in the distance. General Sharaya wiped the sweat from her brow and looked in horror at the oncoming fleet of deylai.

"All of this was just the beginning; a mere distraction. Felanthiam, Augustus, both of you and Commander Niran must round up the remaining soldiers and retreat to the palace now! Mancai has come. My remaining Fairish guardians and I will hold the line until you have reached the palace, then we will fall back and join the defense. Now go!"

Felanthiam turned and saw Mancai's chariot racing towards them.

"Fall back! Fall back to the celestial palace! Follow me!" commanded Felanthiam.

Felanthiam, Augustus and Commander Niran raced back to the celestial palace leading the pack of the remaining, Tanatoors and Theptums. General Sharaya watched Felanthiam lead the way back to the celestial palace then turned to face the Fairish guardians at her side.

"Guardians of the Fairish legions, stand your ground! We will stand strong against the black chariot flames of the destroyer.

Our war cry this night is kayacum no ai, for soon Mancai will be conquered. Soon he will be no more!"

The guardians of the Fairish legion roared in agreement and chanted,"Kayacum no ai, kayacum no ai, kayacum no ai!"

"We will be victorious this great night! Now raise your golden bows and fire your arrows lit with star fire into the hearts of our enemies!" commanded General Sharaya.

The Fairish guardians shot their flaming arrows into the sky, but nothing seemed to stop the chariot racing towards them.

"Let the Fairish Maji's come forward and use their wands!" General Sharaya shouted.

The Maji's that were highly skilled in the ways of Fairish magic flew forward with their wands and began to build an invisible barrier of protection with their magic. The chariot of black flame grew closer and closer until it flew straight into the force field. The sound of Mancai's voice chanting incantations made even the Fairish Maji's tremble.

"Hold the line! Do not let him move you," General Sharaya yelled.

General Sharaya used her wand to make the force field even stronger. Mancai held out his right arm, and his voice echoed across space and time. The Fairish Maji began to fall slowly and painfully one at a time from the crushing weight of Mancai's dark power. General Sharaya looked behind her and saw that the Royals were almost safe inside the celestial palace walls.

"Do not listen to the sound of his voice!" General Sharaya shouted.

"Kayacum no ai, my sisters and brothers! Kayacum no ai!"

The Fairish guardians began to chant once more, even

though more and more of them were killed by Mancai's incantation. The guardians that remained watched their fallen brethren float off into deep space. The sudden roar of a dragon renewed their strength, and the light of Proxima Centauri blinded Mancai.

"Retreat, all of you, and return to the celestial palace at once! The deylai have surrounded us!" shouted Proxima.

"Guardians, you heard the Prince. Follow me and retreat to the celestial palace!" yelled General Sharaya.

General Sharaya and the Fairish guardians lowered their wands and flew with haste to the celestial palace. Prince Proxima Centauri and his unit battled against Mancai, but the strong wizard upheld his right hand and pushed them back. Deylai soldiers flooded through the first quadrant and continued to surround the celestial palace.

"Arokayans, fight them from above!" Proxima shouted.

The Arokayan stars flew above Mancai and reigned fire from their star staffs on Mancai and the deylai army, but nothing seemed to stop their advancement. As Mancai and the deylai drew closer to the palace gates, the fighting squadrons stationed at the celestial palace began to attack. Felanthiam, Augustus and Commander Niran flew to meet Proxima.

"Proxima, Epsilon has told us what the weakness is in Mancai's magic. We must get to him before he finishes the entire incantation or else we are lost. He is trying to conjure the spirit of Ranis to cross over into our heaven. If he succeeds, our entire realm will be under Mancai's control."

"But how, Felanthiam? The deylai protect Mancai," asked Proxima.

"We need all of the six magical forms of light that we wrote in each of our star scrolls to launch an attack on him in unison. I must find Orion, Rigil, and Arev. We need them in order to launch this attack," said Felanthiam.

"Arev has been captured. We may not be able to find him in time, my Queen," said Commander Niran.

"He is here Niran, I can feel it. Epsilon said that Mancai has found a way to increase his power by having a power source with him in battle. Don't you see? This is why he has taken Arev prisoner and why he is so powerful in this battle. Arev is here and close to Mancai. Mancai is draining Arev of his power and using him to fuel his own magic. You must start the assault on Mancai while I find the others. Let the power of celestial fire rain down on him and do not stop until the battle is won!"

"Alright, sister. Go in safety and return in haste."

High King Augustus clasped his beloved sister's hand and then turned to start the assault on Mancai. King Augustus and Prince Proxima flew high above Mancai's black chariot, and used their star staff's to rain star fire upon Mancai. Felanthiam searched for Orion and Rigil first. She found them battling dey-lai star flyers high above the castle, on the northern side.

"Orion and Rigil! Fall back and join King Augustus and Prince Proxima. We have found a way to defeat the sorcerer!"

Orion and Rigil cheered and started to fight their way to Mancai's black chariot. Felanthiam flew high above the castle to get a better look at the black chariot with Commander Niran by her side.

"My Queen, look! The Martians have found a way through the abisynian star fields," said Commander Niran.

"Niran, you must warn King Zionous. Go quickly!"

"Yes, my Queen."

Commander Niran raced to the wall to warn King Zionous of the Martian attack at the rear of the castle. Felanthiam remained high above the castle and watched the chariot of black flame. Smoke surrounded it and she could not see it clearly. She leaned closer to her mighty celestial dragon King Ammon.

"Ammon, beat your mighty wings and clear away the smoke."

King Ammon beat his large scaly wings ferociously and created a powerful solar wind. The smoke around Mancai's chariot began to diminish.

No, it can't be, Felanthiam thought to herself.

The mother of all stars turned and saw the Tanatoorian pirate ship sitting in the courtyard and flew swiftly to it.

"You there, Captain. Can you sail this ship?" asked Felanthiam.

"I can sail this 'ere vessel to heaven's end an' back, I tell yeh!" said Captain Naman.

"Quickly, gather your crew and follow me—but beware. I am sending you all into the mouth of darkness."

Captain Naman laughed wildly.

"My crew an' I 'ill sail to the lowest heavens fer yeh, my Queen. Come on, gents. We'll feast on eye of Kraken this night! Now hurry yer long johns yeh scoundrels, fer we journey into the abyss!"

The mighty wooden ship creaked as it lifted from the ground and followed the Queen of all stars on her celestial dragon.

"Captain, I want you to sail straight into that chariot of black flame and attack the sorcerer," commanded Felanthiam.

"Yeh 'eard her, gents. Now fire yer cannons at will an' full speed ahead!"

Felanthiam joined Augustus, Proxima, Orion, and Rigil in the assault on Mancai just as the Tanatoorian ship crashed into his chariot. The growing power crippled Mancai, and he was tossed out of his chariot.

"Beat your wings Ammon and clear away the smoke and ash!" shouted Felanthiam.

King Ammon beat his wings and the smoke cleared. Felanthiam flew underneath the chariot and found Arev bound underneath and weakened from his power being drained.

"My son! I knew you were alive. You must muster all the strength that you have left in your body and contribute your magical form. We must fight as one to beat Mancai!"

Felanthiam untied Arev quickly and flew him to the others. Deylai star flyers caught onto Mancai, and rushed him back to his chariot. Mancai did his best to complete his incantation, but his power was fading.

"Together, my son. Now!"

Felanthiam and Arev together rained celestial fire on Mancai along with Proxima, Rigil, Orion and Augustus. The six magical forms of the heavens of light were now one.

The Last Stand

The Martian soldiers crawled through the Abisynian star fields with ease. Fairish guardians, royal celestial guards, Theptums and Tanatoors ran to protect the rear of the castle. Although Mancai had been defeated, the deylai came to his rescue and carried him from the battlefield wounded. Fighters from every part of the universe all fought as one and drove back the deylai, but the Martians began to attack the rear.

The roar of the Martian warriors echoed through the tower. Duchess' heart pounded, and she tried hard not to drop her sword. Arokayan soldiers and King Zionous stood ready to fight and even give their lives to protect the last scroll of light. Theptum soldiers from the Tanatoorian aquamarine launched water capsules that stuck to the Martians' heads and drowned them. The swift and crafty Martian soldiers kept advancing and began to crawl up the tower walls like spiders. The soldiers of the Arokayan guard shot star fire from their staffs, but the strong Martian soldiers were many and quickly overwhelmed them. Duchess heard footsteps on the staircase to the tower, and General Sharaya and her Fairish guardians burst through the door—dragging Measles and Popcorn behind them.

"These clowns were hiding like cowards in the courtyard. They will stand and fight here in this tower. Get to your feet, clowns. Guardians, get the King and Duchess out of here and back to Eucharon now. Barricade the door quickly," General Sharaya ordered.

Despite King Zionous' explosive disagreement, the Fairish guardians quickly latched onto him and flew him out the window of the tower straight into the sky.

"I will not leave you, Cousin. I will not leave you to fight and die for us."

"You must leave now, Duchess, before it's too late. Guardians take her!" shouted General Sharaya.

The Fairish guardians latched onto Duchess, but the

Martian warriors started to climb through the window and attack them.

"Stand and fight, all of you! Stand and fight! Protect the Princess and the scroll!" shouted General Sharaya.

The Martian warriors attacked the Fairish guardians, and the Arokayan soldiers fought them with their star staffs.

"We got no other chance now, Pop. Grab this sword 'ere an' swing like yer life depends on it!"

Measles and Popcorn swung their swords wildly, but the Martian soldiers overwhelmed them. A huge Martian made it through the window and fought fearlessly against the Arokayan soldiers. He spotted the clowns and headed straight for them. Measles yelped and tried to run, but the Martian caught him by the neck and lifted him above his head.

"I remember you, clown! At last, you shall be mine to feast on this night!"

"Commander Zebdu? I beg mercy, sir, please 'ave mercy on me poor soul!" begged Measles.

Commander Zebdu turned around and suddenly dropped Measles to the floor when another Martian soldier held up the Arokayan star scroll and yelled in the Martian language. Duchess ran towards the soldier with her sword raised, but Commander Zebdu intercepted her advance and knocked her down. He raised his tri-spear to kill her, but General Sharaya flew to her defense and fought the strong Martian Commander. He overpowered her, and with a quick swing of his tri-spear, General Sharaya fell to the ground lifeless. Commander Zebdu and his warriors roared in delight and jumped out of the window with the star scroll in hand. Fairish guardians flooded into the tower and fought the remaining Martian warriors until all fell silent in the tower, and only the sound of the heavy breathing of the soldiers that surrounded General Sharaya and Duchess could be heard. Despite the faint sound of cheers in the distance of the battle being won, Duchess held her cousin in her arms and wept.

"All is lost."

* * *

Mancai lay weak and dying in the methelem pool of healing waters in the temple of Iona Draconis. Vangemtra rushed to his side and knelt beside her father.

"Rest, my father. Even though today the battle was not won, the thirteen heavens will be one. These healing waters will restore your strength."

Mancai heaved in pain as he tried to speak.

"It...is ours...then?"

"Shhh...just rest, Father. And yes, the Arokayan scroll of the Centauries is ours. We can now seek out and unlock the thirteenth scroll with my blood, right here in our temple."

Glossary

Ahalayum | *A-ha-lay-um* | The Fairish call to summon their wings in the Faree clan. Each Fairish clan has their own call that is spoken in an ancient celestial dialect, that is the Fairish tongue.

Capricornus Constellation | *kaepri-korn-us* | The ancient constellation where the high celestial palace is located in the first heaven—where Felanthiam and Augustus Celenamis rule.

Amarok | *Am-a-rock* | Amarok is King of the arctic wolves that live in Crystal Valley. The ancient ancestors of the arctic wolves live on the frozen planet of Murathim. Long ago, the wolves volunteered to send a pack of their best fighters to earth during the old wars and their descendants still patrol Crystal Valley to this day.

Ammon | *Am-mon* | Ammon is the King of the celestial dragons who were born of star fire upon the creation of the heavens of light. The celestial dragons live in the world between earth and sky.

Black Gateway of Zenith | *Zee-nith* | The Black Gateway of Zenith is a black hole that links the Laniakea universe (where earth is) with the Arokayan universe in the first heaven.

The Council of Crepusculum | *kre'-pus-ku-lum* | An ancient assembly that combined both high celestials, and forces of light and darkness in all of the thirteen heavens. This council disbanded when the tension between Loxidor and Augustus could not be contained and was replaced by the celestial alliance that Epsilon was expelled by. Mancai was cast out by Augustus during the time of this council.

Black Heavens/Dark Heavens/Lower Heavens | The black heavens and dark heavens refer to the lower heavens, which are the six heavens of darkness in the thirteen realms. The heavens of light occupy the first six realms, and the heavens of darkness occupy the lower six. The lowest heaven (or realm) in existence is the thirteenth heaven also known as the great abyss. This was the first realm ever to exist where light was born.

E-may-a-o | Means "Soon we'll be home" in the ancient celestial language.

Felay Menaya | *Fee-lay Men-aye-ya* | The Faree clan call for their wands in the Fairish language. It means "We call forth the gift of magic that the mother of all stars has graciously given to us."

Fiaca Vexme-Drago | *Fee-a-ka Vex-may Dra-go* | A demonic oath of power that the demon armies of Haknami in the seventh heaven take before entering into battle.

Haknami | *Hak-nam-ee* | The planet of Haknami is the place where the demons that dwell in the seventh heaven have built their fortress.

House Grimorie | *Grim-more-ee* | The House of Grimorie is the most powerful house in Witch Kingdom and was founded by Masca Grimorie, who became the eternal High Priest at the temple of Iona Draconis. The House of Grimorie is now led by his descendant Mercuriel.

Iona Draconis | *I-o-na Dra-cone-is* | The dark deity Iona Draconis is believed to be the darkness that covered the universe before time and space came to be.

Kote-uchi | *Co-tay-ooch* | A Kendo form of striking to the wrist in sword fighting in order to disarm an opponent.

Kayacum No Ai | *Kai-a-cum No Aye* | A Fairish warcry that means soon our enemies will be conquered.

Leinani | *Lay-nani* | An aquatic planetary system in the aquanotic region of the third heaven. The third heaven was where the Tanatoors and Theptums moved after Milandria was destroyed by Mancai. The aquatic planets are made up almost entirely of water. Planets in this region are Muriel, Araxia, Dorianna and the aquatic planetary system of Leinani along with the Cantarian galaxy.

Lyanthra | *Lie-an-thra* | Lyanthra is the resting place of the spirit of Ranis. In the ancient days, the thirteen realms were ruled by the great spirits. Ranis ruled the twelfth heaven until the fairies and high celestials imprisoned him on Lyanthra.

Mun Haya Nanoee | *Moon-hi-a Na-no-ee* | The Fairish

interpretation is, "Let the light of heaven guide you back to the ones you love."

Methelum Pools | *Meth-eh-lum* | The Methelum pools are where the most powerful beings of sorcery and dark magic in Witch Kingdom commune with the dark spirits by using pools of water, and blood that flows from the altar of Draconis into pools made of methelum. The pools are kept by immortal druid priests that make blood sacrifices night and day in order for the pools to be used. Methelum is a stone that is harvested from dead stars that have lost their flame. In the temple of Iona Draconis there are thirteen rooms with miles of Methelum pools for each world in each universe, in all of the thirteen heavens.

Smeargoshen | *Smear-go-shen* | A large Martian animal with six snouts. Smeargoshens are large, pleasant and high-spirited animals that are often kept as Eoban house pets. They unfortunately, are very messy because of the purple mucus that they excrete when they become excited.

Srilinayan Star Fields | *Sril-e-nay-an* | The Srilinayan Star Fields is a cluster of stars located in the Arokayan universe. In the days of old, Mancai opened a portal to the eighth heaven so that the trolls could come through and help him fight the Arokayans. The trolls that came through the portal were slaughtered by Arokayan forces, and their bodies created what is now known as the Troll Fields.

The Ancient Book of the Star of Andeeri | The ancient

writings of the star of Andeeri is a holy book that was told to be the voice of Iona Draconis itself and was written by the dark star of Andeeri. In the days of old this dark star was believed to be Iona Draconis in celestial form, and was worshipped throughout the ninth heaven.

The journey continues in...
The Legend of the Star Scrolls:
The Lost Souls Guide to the 13 Heavens

Join the adventure through space and time at
www.ClownTownAdventures.com

ACKNOWLEDGEMENT

I still remember reading this news headline. "26 Arrested After About 500 Kids Cause Chaos in Downtown Chicago, Police Say." In a city where racial tensions run high, the news of hundreds of children wandering helplessly broke my heart. Hopelessness is real and manifests itself in a variety of ways. The massive political and racial divide in today's America has created a volatile atmosphere for American youth. It's time that we use creativity, curiosity, and imagination to pull us into a new era of hope and opportunity.

My second book in my Clown Town Adventures fantasy fiction series for tweens and teens is a diverse and fearless action thriller that challenges readers to think about influence and stand strong in the face of opposition. In order to rise above poverty, destitution, segregation, bias, and prejudice we have to have a vision to hold on to like the rising of the sun. My hope is that my writing helps those who have no opportunity to see the world of possibilities.

It's the vision of the light that we must hold on to when we walk in darkness.

Tephra Miriam is an avid thought leader, author, graphic artist, photographer, musician, activist, and entrepreneur with a passion for change. Tephra grew up in Albuquerque, New Mexico and moved to Chicago, Illinois when she was 18 years old, where she currently resides. Her search for adventure took her far and wide at a young age, and she continues to mentor, learn, work and speak all over the US.

Tephra is a firm believer in redefining the way we think and live. She is a wellness advocate and often blogs on organizational development, challenging the status quo and creating a holistic work environment. Tephra believes that creating space in your life to play, imagine and dream is vital in problem-solving, stress management and innovation.

As a product of 12 years of homeschooling, Tephra started out at Harold Washington College in Chicago, Illinois before transferring to DePaul University and receiving her Bachelor of Arts degree in Global Communications and a Master of Arts degree in Applied Professional Studies with a concentration in Authorship and Entrepreneurialism.

Made in USA - North Chelmsford, MA
1310348_9781092198165
04.05.2022 0838